The Soldier and the Siren

Shifters of Black Isle #2

LORELEI MOONE

CONTENTS

the Deep
Black Isles
Siren's Rock
the Northern Sea
White Cliff
Hythe Bay
the Post
West Hythe
East Hythe
Mainland
No Man's Range
N
S
E
W

CHAPTER ONE

Liliwen had already lost the argument before even starting, but she had to give it one final try. After all, her entire purpose, her reason for being, was at stake.

"Perhaps if I could learn how to fight. I might be of use. Send me to Siren's Rock to train, please, Father!" she pleaded.

King Weiland merely shook his head and averted his gaze, as Liliwen paced the large coral hall that was the seat of the Merfolk's power. He might be content sitting there on his throne, but Liliwen was unwilling to remain a passive bystander. She wanted to *do* something with her life.

What would it take for him to see sense? Why should she waste her talents by sitting around at home, watching, waiting, as the men of the Deep prepared for a battle they were unlikely to win?

Their bloody conflict with the Others who lived on the islands east of their borders had raged on for so long, nobody alive remembered when or how it had all begun. What were they even fighting for?

Actually, the entire situation was stupid. But convincing her father to end the war was even further outside of the realm of possibilities.

"The battlefield is no place for a woman. Why can you not be content with what you have? Leave the fighting to your brother," King Weiland finally replied.

Liliwen rolled her eyes. Why should Cadfael have all the fun, while she was stuck here in what might as well be a gilded cage?

"But, Father!" she argued.

King Weiland looked up at her, and forcefully banged his three-pointed staff into the ground. Its sound bounced around the hall, making the echoes sound a whole lot louder than the original noise.

"That's enough. I will hear no more of it!" King Weiland roared.

Liliwen had no choice but to retreat. The conversation was over.

She looked back once at the elaborate throne, covered in precious stones and shells of all shapes and sizes polished up to a pearly shimmer. Her father still refused to acknowledge her.

Did he think they could go on as they had and still stand a chance to win? If something did not change, they would surely lose.

And without his approval, there was only one thing she could do: take matters into her own hands.

———•◆•———

Liliwen waited in her chambers, determined to follow through on her earlier decision. No matter what her father, the ruler of the Deep, had said, she had her own plans.

As soon as the change of the guard was complete, and the halls of the royal palace were mostly abandoned, she made her move.

"Lili," a voice whispered as she made her way down the hallway. "Hey, Lili. Where are you going?"

Liliwen froze in her tracks immediately. There were few soldiers around at this time of day, but clearly she still failed to move around unseen.

"Cara." Liliwen sighed as she spotted her closest friend waiting in a doorway several feet away from her own. "I'm just going out for a swim. Clear my head."

"Lovely. I'll join you," Cara said. She blinked a few times and smiled one of her most radiant smiles. They'd grown up together and had been inseparable for most of their lives.

Liliwen's heart sank. She couldn't involve Cara in her plans. At least not directly.

She shook her head. "No, I wanted to go by myself."

Cara frowned and brushed a long lock of her golden hair out of her face. "Did something happen?"

Liliwen scanned the hall. There was nobody else in sight, but one could never be too sure. She gestured at Cara to follow her back to her chambers.

Once inside, with the door securely locked behind

them, she finally spoke up again.

"Have you ever felt like you were... I don't know. *More?*"

"I'm not sure I understand. More than what?" Cara asked.

"More capable. More useful. More than what we're being given credit for."

"We're of noble blood. We don't have to work like the commoners. We wear the best fashions and jewelry. And when the time comes, we'll have our pick of eligible bachelors. How much more do you need?" Cara folded her arms and cocked her head to the side.

Liliwen looked down at herself. The elaborate necklace that hung halfway down her chest. The numerous pearl bracelets and gold rings that adorned her hands.

These feelings she'd been battling, they proved harder to explain than she'd anticipated. And dressed up as she was, as was expected of a princess under the sea, her thoughts seemed out of place, even silly.

"But the war... Don't you ever wonder what will happen if we lose?" Liliwen said.

Cara shrugged. "We're safe here. The war happens out there." She gestured vaguely at the door. "It's nothing to do with us. Even if we do lose, do you think those savages are going to come down here and kill us? They can't even breathe under water like we do."

There was no arguing with that last point. Perhaps the enemy wouldn't come down here even if they won.

Perhaps nothing would ever change.

Liliwen wasn't sure whether that was a happy or sad prospect.

"Well, I for one wish to find out what's out there. I want to see what's beyond the Deep."

Cara shook her head. "I don't know why you would. There's nothing there for us. We have all we need right here."

"I'm just curious, alright? These walls are starting to feel like a prison rather than a home. I need space." Liliwen turned her back and faced one of the few windows in her chambers. The view was uninspiring. The same old courtyard of the same old palace she'd lived in all her life. A couple of guards, a few statues of their ancestors, and seaweed.

A whole lot of seaweed in various shades of green, blue and purple.

She'd been stuck here, while Cadfael, her elder brother, was climbing the ranks and making a real difference out there.

What would it be like to go on dry land? Merfolk could do it; that was how they were able to fight effectively even on the enemy's territory. But of course she'd never been outside the Deep. Even Siren's Rock, the Merfolk's land-based training colony, was well out of bounds to her, and that wasn't even far away.

She had tried to run away once when she was younger,

but was quickly recovered by her father's guards. Ever since then, she'd never tried again.

She turned around again.

"You can't tell anyone. Promise me," Liliwen urged.

Cara rolled her eyes. "Just don't do anything stupid."

"I won't." Liliwen hid her lie with a smile. Once she got out there, there was no telling what she would do or how stupid it would turn out to be. But she couldn't sit around in the palace any longer. The outside world was calling, and Liliwen was determined to answer.

——◆——

It was a morning in late spring, stormy, like any other morning in late spring. The clouds hung low, hiding the sun from view. It was only a matter of time before the rains would start.

Overall a gloomy day. Perfect for hunting.

The Reaping was upon them. It had been eight years since the last human had moved onto the Black Isles. And what a long eight years it had been.

Teaq found it hard to think about all the changes his people seen during this time, without feeling bitter about it all. He should have been king. He was the firstborn.

Instead, his younger brother Broc had been crowned seven years ago. And now he intended to take the human as his own, to guarantee himself an heir.

Again, Teaq would be passed over in favor of his

younger sibling.

Not that he was overly interested in taking a bride at this moment, but that was hardly the point. It would have been nice to be considered, at least.

"Sir, the ship is ready. As are the men," someone said, interrupting these dark thoughts of his.

"We'll leave shortly." Teaq gestured to dismiss the soldier, while keeping his gaze fixed on the dark clouds gathering in the distance. One solitary bolt of lightning lit up the sky.

He could have ordered someone else to go on this excursion to the mainland. As General, it was his responsibility to keep the Isles safe from invasion, to command the army in battle and to strategize and strengthen their defenses during times of relative peace. Hunting was not in his job description.

But the truth was, he relished the thought of letting his inner beast loose on the vast plains of the mainland. Hunting had always served as a much needed outlet for Teaq. Nothing cleared the mind like an intense chase. Nothing was as satisfying as returning home with a boatload of wild boar, caught with his own bare hands.

It was a pleasure Teaq and Broc had shared when they were younger, and one of the things the king was forced to sacrificed upon claiming the throne. In a way, Teaq's participation in today's hunt would be all the more enjoyable because of that.

Teaq forced himself into action and made his way down the path leading toward the harbor. A longship was waiting at the furthermost pier, and the hunting party he would lead had already gathered up on the deck.

It was a mixed group; men as well as women, not all of them soldiers, but everyone eager to get their hands dirty. It was a rare pleasure, travelling to the mainland, which had traditionally been their home many generations ago, before the humans had forced them out during the Great War.

The crowd consisted of land animals—predators, as one would expect. Wolves, like Teaq, and bears mostly. The most notable exceptions were the eagles, who would circle the skies as the hunt took place. Lookouts.

Of course, for the moment, everyone was in their human form. But once they got onto the mainland, they couldn't risk being seen. Their truce with the humans forbade them from entering their territory. The islanders were simply too large to be mistaken for fellow humans.

Luckily their animal side would enable them to disguise their presence during the hunt. It also made it unnecessary for them to carry weapons ashore.

"Ready?" Teaq called out as he boarded the ship.

The captain—the only fox on-board—nodded. "Yes, General."

"We'll sail to the White Cliff," Teaq ordered.

"Raise the sail! Rowers, take your positions!" the captain shouted.

Teaq closed his eyes and took a deep breath of salty sea air. It smelled of opportunity, but also of a looming threat.

They were not a seafaring people by origin, but by necessity. Still, they had adapted fairly well in the centuries since they'd taken up residence on the Black Isles. The water didn't bother them anymore. Neither did the harsh climate.

Farming was an impossibility on the Isles, but most of its residents preferred meat or fish over vegetables anyway.

Indeed the islanders' biggest struggle wasn't their own, but the continuing conflict with the Sea Folk, who considered the Black Isles part of their own territory. It was this ongoing war that made today's hunting expedition twice as dangerous.

Not only did they risk the truce with the humans on the mainland if they were discovered, they also had to be on the lookout for Sea Folk soldiers who might try to ambush them along the way.

It was these and similar thoughts that occupied Teaq as the longship started to cut through the choppy waters. He studied the expressions of the remaining hunting party, only to find that they were a lot less thoughtful than himself, and a lot more excited.

Obviously they were looking forward to spending a few hours on a land much more vast than their own. He was too. But as General, he didn't have it in him to ignore the dangers that lurked all around.

So he turned to face forward, his hand firmly gripping the butt of his sword, and scanned the waters for any sign of the enemy.

Until finally, two hours into the journey, the stark white cliffs of the mainland came into view.

iliwen had swum for miles, further and further away from the palace she'd called home all her life. She had made sure to avoid areas that she knew would be heavily guarded, Siren's Rock especially. So instead she found herself traveling east.

Nothing about her surroundings looked familiar anymore. But getting lost wasn't a risk she needed to concern herself with. She, like all of her people, possessed an immaculate sense of direction. No matter how many times she'd change course, she always knew in the back of her mind where home was. She'd find her way back with ease.

At first, she'd felt anxious, be it for another reason. Had someone noticed her departure? Would she be intercepted and taken back home just like all those years ago?

After her earlier disagreement with her father, the punishment for her act of rebellion would be unpleasant to say the least. The King under the Seas could be harsh when his authority was being challenged. He wouldn't let a small detail like Liliwen being his only daughter discourage him from dishing out justice. Even Cadfael, who'd always had a soft spot for his baby sister, wouldn't be able to shield her from that.

But as the time passed, Liliwen felt calmer and more self-assured. She had been stealthy enough to slip away unseen. For once in her life, she was completely alone.

And the views that accompanied her journey were indescribable.

Schools of colorful fish darting through exotic coral reefs as far as the eye could see.

The water even smelled different here. Fresher, crisper.

She didn't just stay down by the ocean floor either. In her eagerness to discover as much as she could, she swam closer and closer to the surface, hoping to catch a glimpse of the kind of creatures who lived beyond the sea, but which she had only ever heard of in stories and song.

Birds. Seagulls.

There weren't any out in the open sea, at least not on this day.

But Liliwen did not let that discourage her. She kept going, until the landscape changed dramatically once again. A huge black granite landmass came into view. It grew upwards out of the ocean floor and rose steeply, extending up and out of the water. She had never seen anything as imposing in her life.

"An island," Liliwen whispered to herself, as she tried to catch her breath.

Having come so close to the Other World, she could not stop herself from exploring further.

Sure enough, the winged creatures she had wanted to see earlier were plentiful around the shoreline. She approached the island and made her way up to the surface, mesmerized by the way they moved through the skies. Flapping their wings, up and down, diving and soaring effortlessly through the air.

It was the most beautiful thing. How were they able to do that without being in the water, she had no idea.

Liliwen knew she should be careful. The Others would be on the lookout for incoming Merfolk intruders. But her curiosity spurred her on to explore more and more of this foreign land. In any case, it seemed like nobody was watching.

———◆———

The hunting party had been a success. Teaq felt a great sense of accomplishment and calm as their ship started on its return journey. Although he still wasn't thrilled about the Reaping, at least the feast would be lavish. They had all the supplies they could have hoped for.

Of course, his own efforts had accounted for a fair share of the wild boar caught by the islanders today. And the after effects of letting his inner beast out and running across the vast plains of the mainland were still raging through his body. His heartbeat was still elevated. His senses were heightened as though he was still in his wolf form.

This high which followed any hunt would last for

another hour or so at least. Exactly this feeling made hunting such a satisfying pastime. One which Broc, his little brother, could no longer partake in.

Teaq scanned the boat. His hunting mates were in a similar state of ecstasy. Each one of them looked content with their respective achievements, even the eagles, who had only served as lookouts. Hunting offered all the thrills of battle, with very few of the dangers.

After adjusting his armor and sword, Teaq forced his attention back toward the waters. They had managed to keep their presence on the mainland a secret, but they weren't home safe yet.

Luckily the two hour return journey passed without incident. They made it back to the Eastern Isle with plenty of daylight to spare.

As the unloading began, Teaq decided to take some moments for himself. He went for a walk along the mostly neglected fortifications along the desolate easternmost side of the island.

Dark clouds hung low on the horizon, promising an upcoming storm. Bad weather was common this time of year and not something the islanders ordinarily had to worry about.

The diffused light and dramatic skies gave the entire island a wild and untamed look. Like nobody was meant to be here. They were only living here on borrowed time.

Would the Black Isles survive the next Great War? Only time would tell.

The Soldier and the Siren

A shimmer just under the surface of the waters down below caught Teaq's eye. He grabbed for his sword and took a step forward, when he found himself face to face with the most unusual creature.

Her silver hair floated gently in the water, framing her heart-shaped face. Her eyes widened as she spotted him, but neither he nor she made a move initially.

She was unlike anything he'd ever seen. A Sea Folk female.

Mesmerized, all he could do was stare as time seemed to slow to a crawl.

Teaq tore himself away for just a second and checked his surroundings. There was nobody else within view. The two of them were completely alone, with only a handful of circling seagulls keeping them company overhead.

He climbed over the wall and onto the rocks lining the shore and got onto his haunches just beside the water's edge.

She did not move an inch initially.

But then, within the blink of an eye, she swam all the way up to the surface.

"Well I'll be damned," he mumbled, in awe of her agility and grace.

With her head and shoulders up out of the water, he could get a better look at her. Everything about her was beautiful. From her silver hair, to her shimmery skin and eyes that shone like pure gold. Her slender body was adorned with all sorts of trinkets and jewelry. Pearls, shells and precious stones. These were all unfamiliar sights on one of her kind.

As far as Teaq knew, no one on the Isles had ever seen a Mermaid before.

After countless battles with her male counterparts, Teaq knew very well that she was one of the enemy. The similarities were undeniable. He knew he ought to capture her. After all, she was clearly a spy sent in to distract and confuse. A new tactic to give the other side an edge in a conflict that had raged on for generations.

But she had neither armor nor weaponry. She was completely defenseless.

Teaq did not believe in chivalry as such, but even he couldn't justify attacking an unarmed female, no matter what species she belonged to.

"What is your business here, Mermaid?" Teaq asked. His voice was not as firm as he would have liked it to be.

She blinked a few times and cocked her head to the side as though she was hearing spoken words for the very first time. That did not make any sense, though. Teaq had exchanged enough slurs and threats with soldiers of the same species to know this.

"I know your people speak our language," he said. "Why have you come here?"

She averted her gaze and coyly brushed a lock of her wet hair behind her ear. A hint of a smile was playing on her shapely lips.

How very human she looked, and yet so alien as well.

"I…" she began to speak. The sound of her voice shook Teaq to his core. It was lyrical, as though she wasn't talking, but rather singing her words.

Even she looked shocked when she met his gaze again, but then quickly recovered.

"I just wanted to see the birds," she said.

Her answer was ludicrous, of course. See the birds. Teaq looked up at the seagulls that continued to circle overhead, no doubt looking for their next meal in between the rocks surrounding them.

"And you specifically came to the Black Isles to see them? Why should I believe you?" Teaq demanded.

He wanted to be firm with her, to do his duty as a protector of the Isles. But he was unable.

"It's so beautiful here. Unlike anything I've ever seen," the mermaid said.

Her eyes were still fixed on his. Within them, Teaq thought he could see truth. Not that that made any sense either.

Although the Elders had learned a great deal about the Sea Folk over the years—the way they fought to the death, showing neither remorse or fear—there was precious little known about their females. Ancient songs told of their beauty, which was evident in front of Teaq right now. But that was all.

Every ounce of sense Teaq still possessed told him he

should be suspicious of this creature. That she was trying to trick him. But his heart couldn't accept it.

"If you think this place is beautiful, tell me of your land, so I may judge it for myself," Teaq said.

The mermaid smiled briefly, then raised herself up out of the water and sat on top of a smooth rock just a couple of feet away from Teaq. If he reached out, he would be able to touch her easily. It was as though she wasn't even trying to evade capture.

"It's mostly seaweed, really," she said.

Teaq couldn't suppress a chuckle, which in turn made her giggle as well.

The voice of an angel.

"Well it's mostly rocks, here."

"I like these rocks. They have depth," she said as she patted the smooth, black stone that currently served as her seat.

They shared an intense look that made Teaq's skin hot and cold all at the same time.

"You're a soldier," she said.

Her tone was firm. It wasn't a question, but rather, a statement. As such, Teaq did not feel the need to answer or correct her, though his position as General was one he held with great pride.

"My brother is a soldier too," she continued. "But he doesn't have so many scars."

They remained silent for what felt like forever. So many unspoken truths between them.

The Soldier and the Siren

Teaq knew how Sea Folk soldiers fought. All or nothing. If he met her brother in battle at some point in the future, likely only one of them would survive.

The way she looked at him, he knew that she was thinking the same as well.

Yet somehow, these horrors did not seem to matter. They had connected, no matter how brief this meeting might end up being.

Her presence here today had awoken something in Teaq. A flame that would prove impossible to extinguish.

CHAPTER THREE

◆

iliwen hadn't planned on getting so far into enemy territory. In all her excitement, she had gotten carried away.

And once she was discovered, that meant there was no turning back at all. She would have been captured if she'd tried to run, so her instincts told her to do the exact opposite. Perhaps she could enchant him, just like the sirens of old.

The man was so different from everyone she knew. Yet it was so easy to turn on her charm for him.

A soldier, like Cadfael, and yet completely and utterly different.

As soon as she'd emerged from the water, her senses became overwhelmed by smells and sights she could not have foreseen. Dry land felt weird. Her skin prickled in the air, making it hard to put up a calm front. There was a current of sorts as well; Liliwen supposed it was called a wind. Much colder than the surrounding air, and very… dry.

And the man. He smelled earthy and spicy and completely incomparable to anything she'd smelled before. Liliwen could not get enough of it.

It was a bit of a chore to hide her excitement and play coy. The latter was especially important if her plan was to work. At least he seemed to want to talk to her, rather than catch her.

"Why have you come here?" he asked.

A fair question. She wasn't quite sure, now that she thought about it. It would be best to keep her answer simple.

The Others had magical powers; legends were told of how they fought. They could shape shift into other beings and often did so in battle. That gave them an edge the Merfolk did not have.

Liliwen knew very well that if this man wanted to, he could transform in an instant and kill her. She knew what he was. A wolf. Every time she closed her eyes, she could see his true form clearly in her thoughts.

"I just wanted to see the birds," Liliwen answered. Although it wasn't the whole truth, it wasn't technically a lie either.

The sound of her own voice was so different out of the water, it startled her at first.

It didn't seem to startle him though. And as silly as her answer sounded, he seemed to be amused by it, which only encouraged her further.

They chatted a little, forgetting for just a moment that they were meant to be sworn enemies.

Finally, after the conversation had died down for a moment, Liliwen felt compelled to take things just a little further.

She raised her arm and reached out for him, brushing her fingertips across his arm. How strange he felt.

Her own skin was flawless, a blank canvas of flexible scales, whereas he was covered in marks. It looked like it would be rough to the touch, but nothing could be further from the truth. So soft, so delicate was his skin.

She quickly pulled her hand back and looked up at him to gauge his reaction. He didn't seem to mind it.

"Your skin is very strange," she observed.

The man grinned and shook his head. "Not from where I'm standing."

Although Liliwen's curiosity was far from satisfied, she knew she'd better quit before she got herself into real trouble.

"I'd better go now." Liliwen smiled briefly, and felt her heart surge when he responded in kind.

It was kind of fun, flirting. She hadn't tried it before, because she'd never found anyone interesting enough to try it with. But his reactions told her that she was more than a little talented at it.

"That's probably for the best," he said.

After one last moment of eye contact, she slid back into the water.

He wasn't coming after her.

She smiled to herself, then swam as fast as she could. What a day. What an adventure!

Cara had made her promise not to do anything stupid. And precisely this promise had been broken in the most grandiose way. 'Stupid' wasn't quite strong enough to describe what had happened today.

And yet…

Her little outing away from the palace couldn't have gone any better. She had truly broken free from her little domain and seen the world.

What would her father say if he found out she'd been talking to one of the Others? A soldier, no less.

———◆———

Liliwen's heart was still pounding when she made it back to the palace. She'd swum at full speed, but the exertion hadn't sent her heart racing. It was the unexpected encounter with the Other. The man-wolf. Or should that be, wolf-man?

She had come so close to being caught. But the threat of capture hadn't really spooked her. It was the man himself.

Tall, broad, more muscular than any Merman warrior. His eyes, an unfamiliar brown that seemed to reveal unspeakable depths and secrets.

He'd made her skin crawl, though not in a bad way.

Every time she blinked, she could still see him in her mind's eye.

The soldier.

A man unlike any other.

The scars on his skin told her he'd seen many a battle.

He had survived, even thrived. How many of her people had he killed? She wasn't sure she really wanted to know.

And yet, he'd let her live. He'd even let her go back home.

A knock on her door startled her.

"Yes?" she called out, trying her best to keep her voice steady. Had her father found out about what she'd done and sent someone to summon her?

Cara burst in. "Lili! You're back. Praise Poseidon."

Liliwen quickly recovered. "I wish you'd stop with those silly superstitions. Yes, I'm back."

Cara grinned. "I'm only teasing you."

Liliwen sat down on her bed and folded her hands in her lap.

"So… where did you go? What did you do?" Cara asked.

There was no way Liliwen could share what had happened. It was too risky.

But how could she keep it all to herself?

She brushed away Cara's question. "Oh… I just swam for a bit. It was very refreshing."

Cara eyed her suspiciously. It was making Liliwen feel uneasy.

"You don't look refreshed. You look like you've seen a ghost," Cara observed finally.

Liliwen looked up at her best friend and pressed her lips together. Should she? Could she risk it?

"You'd never tell on me, if I shared a secret?" Liliwen

asked. Her heart had never quite stopped pounding ever since she'd reached her chambers.

"Of course not. I didn't tell anyone that you left either."

"Promise?" Liliwen cocked her head to the side and studied Cara's features. There was no sign of deceit or ill will in her expression. Not that Liliwen could see, and she'd always been rather good at reading her friend and confidante.

Cara nodded solemnly.

"Fine. I swam all the way to the Black Isles."

Cara's eyes went wide in shock. "No! Why would you do such a thing? What if someone had seen you? They could have taken you prisoner, or worse, just killed you on the spot!"

Liliwen averted her gaze. Someone *did* see her. The reality of just how close to death she had come today was starting to sink in.

And yet… Being in the wolf-man's presence had not made her feel like she was in danger at all. As soon as she realized that he wasn't going to attack her, she had wanted to see just how close she could get to him.

And in doing so, she had *touched* him. She had touched a man other than her brother or father, without first being betrothed to him. That in itself was forbidden. And considering who, or what, the man was…

As Cara had pointed out earlier in the day, she'd never been denied anything in her life. All the treasures of the

Deep were hers for the taking. If she said the word, there would be scores of willing suitors battling each other for the honor of her company.

But that man. That enemy soldier, he was something her father couldn't just give to her. Therein lay the challenge.

If Liliwen wanted him—and she was becoming quite certain did she did—she had to get him for herself. She wasn't a warrior. Her father would make sure she'd never see battle or do anything of note. But *he*... The wolf-man would be her ultimate conquest.

That meant one thing though. Something Cara would not be happy about. Today was only the beginning. She'd have to sneak away more often.

"Hey, are you even listening to me?" Cara demanded.

Liliwen blinked a few times. "Sorry, I was lost in thought. What did you say?"

Cara scoffed. "You're impossible, Lili! I said, promise me you won't go back there. I don't know what I'll do if the Others catch you. I'll die of boredom here on my own!"

Liliwen pressed her lips together. She could promise nothing of the sort.

"But... you don't understand, Cara. Now that I've seen the Islands myself, I have to try and learn all I can about the enemy. I want to help our people, you see..." Of course that last bit was a lie. Liliwen did need to go back. All of her father's guards couldn't keep her away from the

Islands.

Her motives, of course, were entirely selfish.

"You're beyond reason!" Cara complained. "I don't even know what to do with you! Why can't you let things be and let Cadfael and your father worry about the war?"

Liliwen shook her head. "I just feel like I have to do this. Like it's my calling. Does that make sense?"

It was a calling of sorts. The memory of her meeting with the wolf-man was summoning her to go back for more.

Cara shook her head and sat down beside her. "It doesn't. But I suppose I've never had a calling, so what would I know."

Liliwen put her arm around her best friend, rested her head on her shoulder and continued to day dream. It was too bad she couldn't share all she had seen with Cara. Perhaps in time, she'd be ready to speak about *him*.

Silly. He'd had such a huge impact on her after such a short meeting, and she didn't even know his name.

But Liliwen wasn't worried about that. Whenever she'd manage to sneak out of the palace unseen, she'd see him again. She'd go back to the same spot at every possible opportunity, and sooner or later she'd find *him* there. They had an unspoken understanding. She'd seen it in his eyes.

Perhaps he considered her his conquest as well.

Liliwen lay back on the plush pillows that dotted her bed, pulling Cara down with her. There they lay in silence, staring up at the ceiling. Finally, Liliwen's heartbeat began to slow to a more normal pace. And all she could do was smile.

CHAPTER FOUR

e should have caught her. Of course he should have.

Teaq knew he'd made a mistake, technically. But then why had it felt so right to let her go?

Their little encounter had stayed with him throughout the evening. After she'd left, he made his way back to the longship and sailed back to Black Mountain and the castle he called home. Even knowing that there was no chance she'd lingered around all these hours, he still caught himself scanning the waters for any sign of her.

What a magical being. Such beauty and grace. And yet such naivety.

She'd come to see the birds.

Teaq, just like the rest of his people, had lived with a constant threat of war all his life. The Sea Folk were a fierce enemy who could strike at any moment.

They considered the seas to be their domain. And of course, the Black Isles were surrounded by vast amounts of water, which the Sea Folk sought to dominate.

And then this young woman had come along, and told him she'd arrived on their shores just to see the birds.

Had she never seen birds before? He'd never seen a Mermaid before, so perhaps not. Perhaps they didn't travel like their male counterparts did.

Perhaps she'd run off from her own people to go on a little expedition of her own.

She'd seemed enterprising enough, as well as surprisingly fearless for an unarmed intruder. When she'd reached for him and grazed his arm with her fingers, Teaq had wondered for a moment if that was it. If she was hiding some secret weapon or spell that would turn him to dust at her touch.

But actually, she'd just been curious. How laughable. Laughable and in equal measures adorable as well.

He never thought he'd think this way about one of the enemy, but this Mermaid had seemed completely innocent. As if there was no war. And their people hadn't murdered each other over these rocks in the sea for generations now.

But the inconvenient truth was that they had. And what had occurred earlier on the shores of the Eastern Isle while nobody had been watching was an act of treason on both their parts.

Of course, nobody needed to know that.

Teaq was a man of few words usually. Keeping a secret, even one this big, would not be a problem for him. Hopefully she'd be equally discreet and her people wouldn't be on the warpath as a result of their interaction.

As soon as the ship arrived at the Harbor of Black Mountain, Teaq left the crew to their own devices and headed straight for his chambers in the castle. He didn't even see Broc to announce their arrival, or the report on the outcome of the hunt.

All of that stuff suddenly did not seem important anymore.

Teaq, despite his serious, almost cynical nature, was caught in the Mermaid's spell.

He simply could not forget their meeting, however short.

It wasn't just a passing infatuation either. He knew that he would carry these thoughts with him for the foreseeable future. There would be only one remedy: he had to see her again.

Would he, though?

Would she ever come back?

He himself didn't have any reason to return to the Eastern Isle any time soon, and it wasn't even very far for him. She had travelled all the way from the Deep, where the Sea Folk had made their home.

Unusually, he was feeling optimistic. Something told him that indeed, she would make the effort again. And as long as he made sure he returned to that same spot regularly, and kept any nosy onlookers at bay, they would meet again.

———— ♦ ————

Teaq marched into the Great Hall just a bit later than he would have liked. It wasn't in his nature to be tardy.

"Brother, good you are here. Let's begin," Broc said, then turned to face the others who were already present.

The Great Hall was the biggest room within the castle and as such the place where get-togethers, feasts and council meetings were held. Of course, the Islanders never did get very formal, even during official occasions such as audiences with the king. The long benches and tables used for more festive occasions were still placed around the hall in their usual fashion. The Elders sat together on one of the benches, whereas Broc and Teaq preferred to stand. Rhea, their cousin and head of the Royal Guard, along with her second in command, Yorrick, leaned against one of the other tables.

"We have much to discuss," Broc began. "The Reaping. Are we on track?"

Rhea spoke up first. "The castle is as secure as it's ever been. I see no problems."

Her tone was even more gruff than usual. Rhea was obviously unhappy about something. That was nothing new, though. She did not possess what one might call a sunny disposition at the best of times.

"Great. Have someone prepare the chambers near my own for the human's arrival. I intend to keep her close."

"Do you think this is wise, my king?" Rhea asked.

Broc folded his arms. "She might as well get used to my presence from the start, so yes, I do think it is a good idea."

"Might I suggest a guard at her door, at least during the transition?" Rhea asked.

Broc shot her a disapproving look. "She's to be a guest,

not a prisoner. I will not have her treated as one."

"How about you, brother? How did the hunt go?" Broc turned to face Teaq.

"Good," Teaq responded.

Broc continued to look at him, probably expecting some sort of clarification.

What was he hoping for, exactly? A blow-by-blow report?

"We managed to remain unseen by the mainlanders. No problems while sailing either," Teaq added.

"No Sea Folk sightings?"

"No, why?" Teaq responded, then immediately regretted his defensive tone.

"I just want to ensure this Reaping goes smoothly. The last thing we need is for an invasion to hit our shores right in the middle of it all."

Teaq kept quiet this time. It had been an innocuous question. His reaction had been way out of line. This sort of suspicious behavior would get him into real trouble.

"Well, then." Broc turned around and faced the Elders this time. "Uri, do you have anything to add?"

The leader of the Elders stood up and folded his hands in front of his long grey robe. "My king, as you are aware, the last Reaping did not go as planned."

Broc nodded. "I recall that there were problems, yes."

"So we have come up with an idea to minimize these issues going forward," Uri spoke in a thin but commanding voice.

Teaq had no idea how old the man was, but he was certain it was an impressive number. Islanders did not often live to old age. A seat on the Council of Elders was a rare honor only few managed to achieve.

"I'm all ears," Broc said.

"Well, we have decided it would be best if the human is kept in the dark about the true nature of these Isles and their inhabitants, at least during the transition period."

"I'm not sure I understand," Broc said.

"Our powers," another one of the Elders spoke up.

Uri nodded. "Exactly. The human world, although much more vast than our own lands, is also very small in some ways. They do not react well to things they do not understand. As such, we think it is best we introduce any newcomers into our ways gradually. Let's at first make this offering think our ways are much like her own. That way she won't get too spooked."

Broc nodded slowly. "I see. So we pretend to be essentially human."

"That's correct. We advise a ban on transformations in front of the human for the transition period."

Broc remained silent for a moment.

Teaq glanced over at Rhea, who had an even more pronounced scowl on her face now. She was very unhappy about something. It wasn't like her to keep her thoughts to herself.

"Very well. I can see the sense in that," Broc said.

"What if there is an attack though?" Teaq interjected. "I cannot have my men neutered in the face of an enemy invasion."

"Which is also a fair point. Can we agree that there will be no *unnecessary* shifting during the transition period? At least not within the castle, where the human might see? If there's an attack, the ban will be temporarily lifted."

Teaq nodded reluctantly.

Broc turned to get Rhea's input. The latter just shrugged.

"Anything else?" Broc asked.

The Elders shook their heads. Neither Rhea nor Teaq spoke up either. The meeting was over.

Teaq was the first to leave, marching down the hallway toward the stairs. He wanted nothing more than some time alone. After his strange encounter earlier in the day, he had much to think about.

"Teaq," a female voice interrupted. "Teaq, wait up!"

He stopped with a sigh. "What is it, Rhea?"

"This Reaping business. I'm not happy about it," she said.

That much had been obvious throughout the meeting as well. Teaq could only guess what her reasons might be.

"Oh?"

He studied her face. She was visibly tense. The muscles in her jaw were working furiously.

"It's all very well, bringing a human onto our shores for

the survival of our people, but…"

"Our people need the fresh blood." Teaq shrugged. This is how it had been for centuries, whether any of them liked it or not.

"But things are different this time. Broc intends to take her for himself. He's going to have her live in the castle. Unguarded," Rhea complained.

Teaq took a deep breath and folded his arms in front of his chest. "So?"

"So, he's the king. The king's protection is the Royal Guard's main responsibility. *My* main responsibility. It's an unnecessary risk."

"What would you have me do about it?" Teaq asked.

"Speak to him. He's your brother. Make him see the risks involved."

"Do you have any reason to think that this human poses a bigger risk than the previous offerings we've taken?" Teaq asked.

"Call it instinct."

"Could your instinct have something to do with the fact that you wouldn't want to see *any* woman paired up with my brother? Human or otherwise?" Teaq asked.

He didn't care much for gossip or speculation, but even he had noticed that Rhea had developed a liking for Broc. Sadly for her, they were second cousins. The rules forbade any union between partners who were so closely related. There were no exceptions, especially not when the heir of the throne's health was at stake.

Rhea's face darkened even further. If looks could kill…

"I take my job very seriously. And I don't appreciate these kinds of accusations!"

"Fine, fine. I can see how it would be a security risk having a stranger—a human, no less—roam around the castle unguarded. But he's made up his mind already, it seems."

"Just speak with him," Rhea urged.

Teaq sighed. "Fine. But if you want someone to keep an eye on the human once she gets here, you're most likely going to have to arrange for it yourself. Without my brother finding out."

"Right."

She still didn't look happy, but that was as much as Teaq felt like talking about the matter. He had his own problems to think about.

"I'll speak with him," he promised. Then he left Rhea in the corridor and went on his way.

With his younger brother getting ready to take a mate, it was only natural for Teaq himself to consider doing the same. But there was no human girl being shipped in for him. Neither was he interested in one. After today's events, there was only one female he had his eyes on, and she was well out of bounds.

Teaq let out a bitter chuckle as he wondered what the

Council of Elders might say if he sought permission to take a Mermaid as his mate. The rules didn't forbid it. *Technically.*

CHAPTER FIVE

The days passed at a crawl. Liliwen grew more and more restless, the longer she found herself confined to the palace.

She had to slip away again.

Her memories of the brief meeting with the Other stayed with her at every waking moment, and even in her dreams. The longer she stayed away, the less likely it would be that she'd meet him again.

And she really did have to meet him once more. Every fiber in her body screamed for another chance to see him.

Finally, she got her chance a whole four days from her initial excursion. Her father was preoccupied with the upcoming premonition ceremony. As a result even the castle guards had better things to do than keep track of one rebellious princess's whereabouts.

Liliwen told Cara, just because the secret felt too big otherwise. Cara of course tried to discourage her, but Liliwen didn't listen. The urge to see the soldier again was simply too strong.

Once she had slipped out of the palace unseen, she knew exactly where she was going thanks to her impeccable sense of direction. She did not let herself get side tracked by exotic fish or birds flying overhead. Liliwen was heading straight for the island where she had met him the first time.

As soon as the black cliffs came into view, she felt her heartbeat surge again, just like that day.

It was a beautiful kind of thrill. The danger was palpable. How romantic, to risk punishment by her own people, as well as capture by the enemy, just to see a man. If she could catch but a glimpse of him, it would all be worth it, she told herself.

He wasn't there, though. She waited just underneath the surface, in exactly the same spot as last time, for what felt like hours.

The skies were cloudy, though occasionally a ray of sunshine broke through and changed Liliwen's entire outlook. It was only her second outing, so the bright light reminded her that there was still so much for her to discover in this strange land.

She'd never seen sunshine before. It was gorgeous and renewed her hope that today's journey wouldn't be for nothing.

Breaking the surface of the water just for a moment, Liliwen felt the heat of the sun on her skin. It was so warm. The air felt even drier than last time. She quickly went under again, only leaving her head and one raised hand exposed.

"Hey, Mermaid!" a voice interrupted her experiment. "You'd better be careful if you don't want to be discovered."

She turned as quickly as she could.

"You came back!" she exclaimed with a smile.

"As did you." The wolf-man climbed over the fortified wall and sat down on the same rock as the last time.

He stretched out his right arm and dipped his fingers into the water. "Oh, it's nice and fresh today."

"Same old," Liliwen joked.

"You don't have to tell me."

"My name is Liliwen," she blurted out before she had the chance to think whether giving her real name was a good idea or not.

The man paused for a moment. "That's a beautiful name. I'm Teaq."

"Tcaq, the soldier," Liliwen repeated.

The man smiled briefly. Even last time he hadn't given the impression he was the sort of guy who laughed or smiled a lot. And yet here, with her…

It made her happy just thinking about it.

A loud noise filled the air, causing Liliwen to cover her ears. "Oh my, what was that?"

"Just the change of the guard. Nothing to worry about."

"Are there many guards here?" she asked.

Teaq squinted as though her question had raised his suspicions just a little. "Just enough so we'll come to know if something—or someone—tries to approach unseen."

"Aha." They shared yet another, more sensual look.

Liliwen thought for a moment, then decided to go with

a shock and awe approach for this second conversation. He would never see it coming.

"I told my friend that I was going to the Black Isles to find out anything I could to help our cause." Liliwen watched carefully for his reaction to her words.

"Did you?" Teaq folded his arms in front of his chest.

"I lied, though." She smiled, then looked away at the distance. "I mean, what am I going to learn here, anyway? If I make sure I remain far away from the guards, then I can't be spying on them either, right?"

"Indeed… So why did you actually come here? To see more birds?" Teaq asked.

"To see you," she said, lowering the pitch of her voice just a little.

His reaction was obvious. The way his expression softened and his gaze grew more intense. He liked her answer.

Should she leave it at that, or take things just a notch further?

"Are you stationed on this island, or did you come here just for me?" she asked. Although she had tried to keep her tone light and innocent, it was a loaded question.

Liliwen knew exactly what she wanted to hear and anything less would be a great disappointment.

"I think you already know the answer to that," he said.

Oh, what a tease!

She let out a soft chuckle. This game, it was getting easier by the minute.

"You know, I'm not even allowed to be out here." Liliwen caught a stray lock of her hair with her finger and twisted it round and round. Her hair felt weird out of the water. Sticky. She was certain it looked crap too, though the way he continued to look at her suggested he hadn't noticed that.

"I've been wondering about that. We don't get to see a lot of Mermaids around these parts."

Although it was an obvious truth, the fact that she was the first of her kind that he'd ever seen gave Liliwen a thrill.

"My father would be furious if he found out. In fact, I'm pretty sure he'd punish me for swimming off on my own," she continued.

"You don't seem to be the sort who follows the rules," Teaq observed.

Liliwen smiled. "If I'd followed the rules, I would have never met you. And then where would we be?"

"You'd be at home, safe. And I'd be…" His voice trailed off.

Liliwen pouted and looked down at the water below. "So you'd prefer if we hadn't met at all?"

"You'll admit that this—whatever we're doing here—is rather complicated. The risk we're taking if discovered…" He reached out for her. The back of his fingers gently caressed the side of her face, until they stopped just under her chin, and guided her face upward again.

His touch sent shivers down her whole body and took her breath away all at the same time.

"Easy is just another word for boring," she whispered, as she met his gaze.

Just how long could she continue like this? Putting up a calm front, while Teaq was toying with her emotions so effortlessly?

Within a couple of exchanges between the two of them, Liliwen's state of mind had gone from joyful, to hurt and now... Excited didn't quite explain it. His touch had set her alight, and soothed her all at the same time. And yet there were still those nagging doubts just underneath the surface.

He pulled away his hand again, which nearly made her wince.

Don't stop!

Wait, since when did this game turn to his favor instead of hers? She had already become obsessed with him, but was he perhaps just playing with her? Did he not have a stake in this?

"I doubt you'd ever be boring, Liliwen." The way he spoke her name made her even weaker inside. But she was determined not to let it show.

No, she thought, he's as involved as I am. Otherwise he would have simply taken her prisoner by now.

She reached for his hand, and weaved her fingers in between his. So warm, even more so than the sunshine she had encountered for the very first time before his arrival.

Liliwen's thoughts began to wander. What it might be like, to feel more of his touch? How would it feel, to really come together? To connect as man and wife. The ultimate bond. Was he this hot all over?

The same hideous noise from earlier filled the air again. She quickly let go of him and covered her ears for some relief. "Doesn't it hurt your head? This ruckus."

Teaq shook his head. "It's not all that loud. You should hear our war horn."

Liliwen frowned. "I don't think I'd like that very much."

Teaq stood up and scanned their surroundings. "I think it would be best if you went on your way now."

"Is anyone coming?" Liliwen asked.

"It's time for the evening patrol," he explained.

Teaq gestured at her to get into the water, which she did, reluctantly. There was still so much to talk about. There were an infinite number of things she wanted to know about him, which she hardly knew how to ask about.

"I'll see you again," he said.

With a heavy heart, Liliwen nodded. "Soon."

Just how soon she would get another chance to slip out of the castle, she couldn't be sure about. All she knew was that she couldn't bear being away from him for days on end. This little game they were playing had turned very serious, very quickly.

This isn't just a flirtation, Liliwen thought to herself. This… This might be love.

———◆———

"Lili," Cara barged in. "Hey, Lili!"

"What is it?" Liliwen looked up and found Cara in the doorway with wide eyes and an excited grin on her face.

"Cadfael is back!" she squealed. "Just in time for the ceremony, too!"

Liliwen jumped up and took Cara's hands, such was her excitement. "Really? Where is he?"

"He's just entered the throne room to speak with your father. Shouldn't take him too long, I would hope."

"Oh my, I wonder what stories he'll tell this time. Where all he's been. I have much to ask him."

"You cannot!" Cara warned.

"I cannot what?" Liliwen placed her hand on her hip and stared Cara down defiantly.

"You cannot tell him you swam off! You'll be in so much trouble. We both will, since I covered for you."

Liliwen pressed her lips together. "Fine, you're right. But I still have a lot to talk to him about."

Cara smiled. "I'm just glad he's back in one piece."

Liliwen cocked her head to the side and studied her friend's face. "Me too."

"I mean… it's so dangerous out there. I wish he didn't have to go back on patrol."

"Indeed…" Liliwen squeezed Cara's hand.

"Yes?" Cara met her gaze.

"You like him!" Liliwen observed.

Cara instantly looked down at the ground. "I… Well, he's nice and all."

"You *like* like him!"

Cara shook her head. "Don't be silly. Though he is rather handsome."

"Don't be ashamed, Cara. He's a fine soldier, and a kind man as well. You could do a lot worse."

"You mean… Do you think he'd be…?" Cara stammered.

Liliwen shrugged. "Only one way to find out, don't you think? Why don't you talk to your mother, and have her speak with my father about it. See what he thinks?"

"I… Yes. Perhaps I should do that. But I'd like to see *him* first," Cara said.

Liliwen smiled and nodded encouragingly. "Alright. Let's go find him then."

"You don't mind? It's not weird, me with your brother?" Cara whispered.

"We're almost like sisters anyway. What's weird about it?"

"Oh, Lili. Wouldn't it be amazing if this works out?" Cara's voice was heavy with emotion.

Just the thought of the two of them finding love almost at the same time nearly brought tears to Liliwen's eyes. She really ought to say something, share her own story with Cara. But it was too early. Too uncertain. And way too forbidden.

Or could she risk it?

"It would be... Speaking of amazing," Liliwen's voice reduced to a whisper. "Keep another secret?"

"For you, of course!" Cara said.

"Okay, in that case I have something very big to tell you..."

And just like that, Liliwen spilled all. After keeping all these feelings locked inside of her with no one to tell, it felt good to let it out. Even if another person knowing doubled the risk. If Liliwen's father came to know... The repercussions would be huge.

CHAPTER SIX

onight was the night. The Reaping was upon them.

As general of Black Isle's armies, Teaq was onboard the ship sailing to the mainland to collect the newest addition to the islanders' ranks. Broc was also onboard; no matter how hard Teaq had tried to discourage him, his brother certainly had a mind of his own.

This was no place for him though.

And because the king was onboard, Rhea, as his appointed protector and head of the Royal Guard, had accompanied them as well. That meant that on this very ship, the three most important and powerful people of the Black Isles were together at once. An easy target, should anyone wish to attack.

The whole thing was idiotic anyway.

Broc had made up his mind already; he was going to take the human as his queen. And Rhea's concerns, although borne in jealousy, were not completely unfounded. Any newcomer was by their very nature a security risk.

Teaq could have handled the pick-up on his own, along with some hand-picked soldiers and sailors. But instead, Broc was intent on putting himself, and along with it, the stability of the Black Isle's rule, in harm's way.

All for a woman he'd never even seen before.

How he could do such a thing, Teaq couldn't begin to understand.

Teaq and Rhea shared plenty of disapproving looks throughout the journey to the mainland.

Thankfully it was foggy, meaning the humans would not be able to spot them easily.

Sure, the rules of the Reaping forbade anyone from lingering around the shore to watch as the islanders picked up their prize, but humans could be unpredictable. You never knew if this particular one had an unhappy parent or sibling, willing to risk everything for her recovery.

And so, as the ship approached the shore, Teaq kept his eyes fixed on the misty beach for any sign of movement.

"Drop anchor!" Teaq ordered, and braced himself as the ship came to a very sudden halt in the shallows.

He had his hand on his sword as he carefully stood lookout at the bow of the ship.

In the distance, Teaq could just about make out the outline of the post to which the girl had been tied.

"There she is," Teaq grumbled.

"Remember, she will be shown the respect deserving of any citizen of the Black Isles," Broc responded.

Teaq didn't react, only rolled his eyes.

Behind him, Rhea mumbled something unintelligible. She was understandably pissed off as well.

The Reaping only took place once every eight years. One fertile female of marriageable age, picked from one of the villages of the mainland, left alone on this beach for the islanders to claim.

This arrangement was all part of the truce the islanders and the humans had enjoyed for generations, ever since their banishment to the Black Isles at the end of the Great War. So far, nobody had broken it. But one could never be too careful.

For Teaq, this was the second Reaping he had taken an active role in. During the last one, their father, the late king Ryk, had still been around, though he did not come along to pick up the girl herself. He had stayed at the Black Mountain, just as Broc should have done.

"Just remember what we discussed," Teaq grumbled. "These are troubled times. The last thing we need is further complications within our own walls."

Part of Teaq could understand that Broc wanted to be among the first to lay eyes on his new bride, but just why he had taken to the ritual with so much excitement, he couldn't understand. The last time, they'd had a hell of a time getting the girl to adjust to her new life. Teaq, for one, could not stand the kind of drama human females seemed overly fond of. The entire Reaping ritual was an irritating, be it necessary evil.

Mating with humans wasn't by choice. It was a must, to ensure the health of their offspring during times when their numbers had thinned so much that inbreeding became a very serious risk.

Teaq himself couldn't imagine participating anyway. He had his sights set on something much more special than any human. The Mermaid, Liliwen, had made a permanent impression on him. She did not play games like human females. Neither was she blunt like some of the islanders; Rhea included. She was unapologetically and elegantly herself.

"I wish you'd reconsider and at least let me put a watch on her. We do not know of her intentions," Teaq muttered. Some of the things Rhea had said had left a lasting impression on him.

"Alright. That's enough of that," Broc scoffed. "We've laid down the rules already. But I won't have her treated as a prisoner under my rule. Let's get on with what we came here to do."

Teaq shrugged and jumped over the edge of the boat, into the freezing water. The cold didn't bother him. Neither did the harsh winds that swept across the desolate beach.

Broc followed him, as did a few more soldiers.

Once everyone had made it to dry land, they marched straight toward the girl, with Teaq leading the way, his sword at the ready. There was a strange smell in the air; hers, probably.

The small group crossed the distance of the wind swept beach in no time.

"Hold on," Teaq warned Broc, intending for him to stay behind him in relative safety. Of course, his little brother did not listen and stopped right next to Teaq.

"What's your name, girl?" Teaq asked.

The girl, who had obviously not noticed them approaching, let out a shrill squeal, but quickly recovered and spoke her name. Kelly something.

Teaq wasn't even listening anymore.

He undid her ties at Broc's request, but otherwise was preoccupied trying to compare her to Liliwen. The human had striking red hair, but otherwise looked ordinary. She was rather tall for a human, though, so at least she had that going for her. At the very least Broc's heir wouldn't be too short, then.

But she had nothing—absolutely nothing—on Liliwen.

Teaq raised an eyebrow, when, shortly after speaking with Broc, the woman fainted, much to Broc's excitement, who managed to catch her. The guards who had accompanied them weren't much in the way of company. For once, Teaq wished Rhea was here so he could roll his eyes at her and be met with understanding, rather than blank looks.

He breathed a sigh of relief when Broc turned around and led the way back to the ship. There was no use sticking around here any longer than necessary.

As soon as they had climbed aboard with their human cargo, Teaq gave the order to sail back to Black Mountain. They completed the journey almost completely in silence, with a sleeping girl in their midst.

Teaq hoped Rhea would stick to her plan and have the human followed, at least at first. She really had no business wandering the halls of Black Mountain unaccompanied, no matter what Broc thought about it.

———◆———

All through the following day, Teaq walked the halls of the castle in a daze. He hadn't slept, just tossed and turned for most of the night. He hadn't spoken to Rhea to find out what she was doing about the human.

Neither had he done anything about the matter himself.

Never before in his life had Teaq felt so distracted. It was as though Liliwen had cast a spell on him. He might as well go back to the Eastern Isle to wait for her, since that was all he was thinking about anyway.

Of course, sneaking off to the most remote of the Black Isles without rhyme or reason wasn't something a man in Teaq's position could afford.

He was the second most powerful person in the kingdom. The commander of Black Isles' armies and Broc's right hand man. And right now they were in the middle of one of the most significant of the Isles' traditions. They had picked up the human offering from the mainland the preceding night, and as such the Reaping had begun.

It wasn't just a cause for celebration for whoever would claim the human bride; Broc, in this case. It was also an event the entire Isles looked forward to. An excuse for a rare and lavish feast that would last for five entire nights.

This was what Teaq and the others had been preparing for. They had stocked up on meat from the mainland, as well as ale, wine and any other treat the islanders normally wouldn't indulge in so much.

Inhabitants of the surrounding islands had flocked to Black Mountain to take part in the Reaping Feast. If there was ever a worse time for Teaq to shirk his responsibilities as the protector of the Isles, this was it.

He and his men would also feast, of course. But they would also stand by in case of any attacks. The thing about being at war with a formidable and unpredictable enemy was that you could never be sure when the next attack happened.

It had been a quiet winter, but the weather had warmed up. Sea Folk were more likely attack in the summer. So they all had to be on their toes.

But instead of inspecting the defenses of Black Mountain, Teaq had been skulking around the empty hallways of the castle, thinking about Liliwen. Thinking about how her skin had felt when he'd touched her. About how being so close to her had made her feel.

These had been the thoughts that had haunted him throughout the night as well.

Considerations of right and wrong hadn't really come into it. In all his interactions with her, he'd relied on instinct. His instincts hadn't told him to treat her as an enemy, no matter what species she belonged to. In fact, his inner beast was shouting the loudest that he should just forget about everything else, and make her his.

How that realistically would work, he didn't know. His rational mind knew that there was no future for them. That this little fantasy would end in tears.

But his heart wouldn't listen. Hence he found it impossible to get out of this funk.

"Hey, there you are!" Rhea's voice startled him.

"What?"

"What's wrong with you? You look like you've seen a ghost," Rhea said.

Teaq quickly recovered. "Just thinking. Never mind. What do you need?"

"I don't need anything. But, the feast is about to start."

The feast... Teaq rolled his eyes.

"It would be odd not to attend, wouldn't it?" Teaq grumbled.

Rhea shrugged. "I don't feel much like celebrating either. But yes, it would border on being insulting not to."

"Well, then. Let's not keep my dear brother waiting," Teaq said.

He led the way through the zig-zagging corridors of the castle, straight to the Great Hall. The festivities inside were already well underway. Crowds and crowds of people had taken their seats on opposite sides of the long tables, chatting excitedly. The food and drink had not been brought in yet.

Teaq and Rhea were meant to sit on the main table next to Broc. One difference compared to previous feasts was the addition of a carved chair beside Broc's throne.

Teaq sighed. So he was expecting the human to join them as well.

Not only was Broc intent on ignoring Rhea and Teaq's warnings about the new addition in their ranks, he would rub their noses in it by seating her right next to him.

Teaq turned and glanced at his companion. Rhea had spotted the new throne as well. Her already grumpy expression had turned hateful as she glared at it.

CHAPTER SEVEN

———◆———

The throne room was fully decked out. Decorations adorned the walls, the furniture, even the throne itself. King Weiland had on his ceremonial robe, along with a crown made of shark's teeth and precious gems reserved just for this occasion.

Liliwen had slipped inside along with the last guests. Hiding out anonymously in the crowd was not an option, unfortunately. Ordinarily she did not mind taking her seat by her father's side, but today, she would have liked to stay out of view.

She had been carrying her memories of her last meeting with Teaq around with her like a heavy burden. Although she'd told Cara about it— the thrill of a man's touch, experienced for the very first time—hiding the truth from everyone else weighed heavy on her.

It wasn't just the journeys she'd made to see him that were forbidden. If it came to light that anyone had made advances on Liliwen, even touched her, her father would likely cut off his hands. If furthermore it turned out Liliwen had been a willing participant, she would be punished for that as well.

And as she made her way through the visiting dignitaries from all over the Kingdom of the Deep, she felt as though Teaq's fingers had left a lasting mark on her face. Like anyone who looked at her closely could see what she had been up to.

Thankfully though, nobody said anything. Cadfael, who was already seated toward the king's right, winked at her, giving her a little more courage.

She made her way up the raised platform and found her own, slightly smaller seat at her father's left hand. Liliwen straightened her back and met the crowd's looks head on as she sat down. Whatever happened, she couldn't show anymore weakness without attracting suspicion. She was a princess, after all. Her position did not give her much power, but it did garner attention.

Oh, how she wished she could just swim away from it all.

King Weiland banged his three-pointed staff on the ground to attract everyone's attention, then got up from his seat.

"My dear citizens, who have traveled far and wide to be with us today on this auspicious day!"

Liliwen scanned the attendees, looking for Cara. Sure enough, there she was, but she didn't notice her best friend at all. Cara was staring unapologetically in Cadfael's direction. Liliwen glanced over to her right, past her father's throne. Cadfael was looking at Cara as well!

So in the short while he'd been back from Siren's Rock, she had somehow gotten his attention.

Liliwen sighed and sat back. Good for them. Not that it

helped with her predicament, though.

"We are gathered here, as we do every two moons before every summer solstice, to consult the currents and predict our fortunes in battle this fighting season."

Liliwen tried hard not to roll her eyes. Not once had she heard a specific and useful prediction during one of these ceremonies. And still, everyone sat through them religiously every single year.

"Bring in the Seer!"

The large double doors at the end of the throne room swung open, and half a dozen priests in ceremonial gowns floated in. In their midst was the Seer. A Merman just like the rest of them, and also unlike any of them. His scaly skin wasn't greenish like Liliwen's kin, but had a grayer, almost bluish tint. His eyes weren't golden, but a stark white. And he had no hair on his head at all.

Baldness wasn't something Merfolk ever suffered from. Except this particular one.

The last of his kind, Liliwen thought. The ceremony was nonsense, of course, but the Seer did creep her out a little.

They said he was the last survivor of a clan of Merfolk who had ruled the Deep before Liliwen's people had even arrived here. Wiped out by some kind of disease that had claimed all their lives. Perhaps that was why he was bald.

Either way, he was meant to have mystical powers, or so people believed.

"My King." The Seer bowed deeply in front of Liliwen's father, who nodded and gestured at him to get back up.

"Let us begin the Premonition Ceremony!" King Weiland said, as he ran his right hand through his long white beard.

The six priests formed a semi-circle around the Seer, who closed his eyes and raised his arms up toward the ceiling.

Drums started to play, adding to the creepy ambience that was specific to this ceremony.

"Great Currents of the Northern Sea. What truths do you carry? What predictions do you have for all our fortunes?" the Seer asked aloud.

The priests began to dance around him to the rhythm of the drums, moving first in a clockwise direction, and then as they completed a whole revolution around the Seer, they returned counter clockwise, to their original positions.

"Tell us, oh powerful currents! Messengers of Poseidon, speak to me!"

He then reached for the large conch that hung from a gold chain around his neck and held it up to his right ear. He aimed it upward at the ceiling.

Liliwen watched the whole thing with mixed emotions. She didn't really believe in any of it. But what if…

"The Black Isles are in trouble," the Seer spoke.

A whisper passed through the crowd.

Liliwen sat up straighter in her seat. This year's

prediction seemed to be a lot more specific than she was used to.

"A stranger, unlike any of them. A stranger will move onto the Isles, changing their fortunes forever. She will turn brother against brother. Soldier against soldier."

The Seer looked straight ahead, his gaze meeting Liliwen's.

Her heart sank. He'd seen it. He'd figured it all out. She was found out. All was lost.

"A stranger, with great power," he continued. "A human, with a secret."

Finally, Liliwen could breathe.

The Seer closed his eyes again. "Oh Poseidon. Send your messengers to us with more predictions. Will we be victorious, oh mighty Currents?"

Liliwen sat back in her seat, trying hard to catch her breath without anyone noticing.

"The stranger's arrival will have them at their weakest yet," the Seer concluded. "The currents have spoken. This is all."

King Weiland got up from his throne and applauded. "Do you hear this, my friends? Poseidon favors us. The Black Isles will tear themselves apart, and we'll attack to make the most of their weakness. Victory shall be ours!"

The crowd roared as the priests moved into a two by three formation and walked out behind the Seer.

"Long live the Deep!" one of the visitors shouted.

"Long live King Weiland!" the entire audience replied.

———— ◆ ————

"This is getting to be a habit," Teaq said with a smile.

Liliwen smiled back at him and slipped her hand into his.

This. This was what she had craved. Despite her scare the other day, during the Premonition Ceremony, she had been unable to stay away.

Although she had confided in Cara, she had been unable to put into words just how he made her feel. These stolen moments, away from the conflict that had raged on between their people. Away from stupid superstitions and predictions.

How she wished she could just stay here forever. But the risks were too great. They were too visible out here.

"Is there somewhere we can go? Somewhere a little less exposed?" she asked, desperate not to have today's meeting cut short like the last time. She had, after all, just swam halfway across the Northern Sea for this. For him.

Teaq turned around and studied the barren countryside.

"There is a place, but it's some way up the hill," he said.

Liliwen followed his gaze. The island looked very different than the ocean floor she had travelled along to get here.

Seaweed provided vast expanses of lush greenery for the fish and many other sea creatures to hide in. This land had none of that. No vegetation. Not even any wildlife. Not another soldier in sight either.

How would she get up there? She'd heard the stories of her people climbing onto dry land to fight, but how it really worked was hard to imagine. She'd never done it before.

It was the only way she'd be able to spend more time here, though…

"Okay, help me up," she said, reaching out for him.

Teaq reluctantly held her by the wrist and gave her a pull. Before she knew it, she was balancing on top of the rock she had only just sat on. He hadn't even broken a sweat getting her out of the water, such was his strength.

It was a challenge staying upright. How did Cadfael and the others do it?

Liliwen looked down at her tail, which was bending awkwardly trying to hold her height. With a bit of practice she might stand on it without any support, but how was one supposed to move around like this?

"Ugh, this is weird." Liliwen smiled awkwardly.

"Where are your legs?" Teaq asked.

Liliwen looked down again. Legs? Had he seriously just asked that?

"What do you mean?" she asked.

"When the Merfolk attack… I mean, your people, when they come here, they can crawl and walk much like what we do. On two legs. Not…"

"Not one flipper," Liliwen mumbled, suddenly very

conscious of her body. "It's useless, isn't it?"

"It's beautiful. You are beautiful," Teaq whispered under his breath, then cleared his throat. "Perhaps it's something only your men can do."

Liliwen frowned. She was just as capable as any man. There had to be a trick to it. She couldn't be handicapped on dry land just because she was a woman. That would be unacceptable.

Unless it was magic. Did her people possess some kind of secret magic she didn't know about? The stories made it sound so natural.

"I can just carry you, if that's acceptable," Teaq suggested.

"Absolutely not. I will go myself," Liliwen argued. *But how?*

With Teaq's hand on her shoulder, keeping her roughly in position, she put all her energy into that all important first step. Or should that be, her first hop?

She gave it her all, and immediately lost balance and fell backwards into the water with a big splash. So much for trying to impress him.

Liliwen was furious when she jumped out of the water again and onto the rock. This time, she was steady.

"Ah, there they are," Teaq observed with a grin on his face.

Liliwen looked down and was shocked to find that her tail had split in two right through the middle. She had legs!

Scaly, like the rest of her, and not quite the same shape as his, but legs nonetheless. And even her tail had come apart and formed two sections to serve as her feet. She shuffled the two halves apart, copying how Teaq was standing, and found that her balance was much improved.

"So this is how it works," she mumbled to herself.

"You know, I never thought about this before. Just how did you do it?" Teaq asked.

Liliwen shrugged, and shook her hair back as a show of confidence. "I'm not sure, but the important thing is, I can go now." His question did play on her mind though. More importantly; how would these two halves merge again for her long swim back? If they didn't, there was no way she could be seen at home without every single person knowing that she'd been up to no good.

She took a deep breath. That was one hurdle she'd have to cross later.

Teaq offered her his hand, which she gladly took as she unsteadily climbed over the rocks toward the boundary wall of the island. He did lift her over the top of it, which she accepted grudgingly. That was better than making a show of herself falling off the damn thing.

The rest of the way up the mountainous island took her a while, but she managed it with Teaq's help. Surely, with a bit of practice, she'd be as comfortable out of the water as any of her male counterparts.

As they made it further up the hill, the place Teaq must have been referring to came into view. A cave, sheltered from the surrounding landscape. The ultimate escape from prying eyes.

Liliwen's heart skipped a few beats as she thought about everything one might get up to in there, without anyone knowing. Had he taken other women there? Or was she the first?

The mystery of not knowing made being here even more exciting.

"Here we are," Teaq said. He stepped aside to let her enter the cave.

It was pitch black, but Liliwen had no trouble seeing inside. In fact it was easier on her eyes than the bright island.

She wandered in, and found herself a suitable place to sit and rest her newly formed legs. Swimming for hours was effortless for her, but this short hike had taken its toll.

Teaq sat down a couple of feet away.

Neither of them said a word initially. The silence between them increased the tension tenfold. It had been her idea to come up here. What were his motives, though? Was he thinking what she was thinking?

"It's nice," she remarked, finally. A meaningless statement, but her nerves wouldn't allow her to stay silent any longer. "Not so dry and windy."

Teaq didn't respond.

She placed her hand on the ground beside her. The entire cave was covered in a soft and springy material. Like a very fine and dense seaweed. Liliwen caressed it, marveling at how the thin sprigs sprung back upright after she'd touched them.

"What do you call this?" she asked and patted the ground, gesturing Teaq to come closer.

"Moss." Teaq got up and joined her. His movements were wooden, as though suddenly he wasn't so sure of himself anymore.

"Moss," Liliwen repeated after him. "Such a cute word."

She looked over at him and wondered what her next move should be. His behavior since they'd arrived in the cave was confusing. Was it all one-sided after all? She had to be sure.

"Why haven't you taken me prisoner yet?" she finally asked, then held her breath as she waited for his answer.

CHAPTER EIGHT

"Why haven't you taken me prisoner yet?" Liliwen asked.

Teaq nearly choked on his own breath. Islanders weren't known for mincing their words. Though Liliwen had been straightforward with him so far, she still continued to surprise him with her candid questions.

"I… Well, that's the question, isn't it?"

"I want to know the answer," she insisted.

He couldn't very well tell her that from their very first meeting, he'd been so fascinated by her that he couldn't bear the thought of missing out on these moments together? That he'd been obsessed with her to the point of not being able to sleep at night. That he'd sat through one too many Council Meeting or discussion with Broc, only listening to half of what was being said, because the image of her, glistening in the diffused light of early summer, had been etched onto his mind permanently.

"I think you're just toying with me," she said, looking down at her hands which were now wrapped around her legs. Or was that her tail? Whatever it was.

"One day when you grow tired of me, I'm going to come visit, and you'll put me in chains."

"Never," he said. His voice sounded more hoarse than normal.

She knew exactly what buttons to press. It was infuriating. And addictive.

"Prove it," she mouthed.

Teaq leaned over, placed his hand on her cheek more firmly than he'd ever touched her before and looked into her eyes. Though the cave was dark, her eyes shimmered golden as usual. It was a beautiful sight to behold.

"I would never."

Liliwen's eyelids fluttered, then shut entirely.

His senses were overwhelmed by her. Her quick shallow breaths sent his own heartbeat into a frenzy. This. This was what he'd been thinking about doing sometime between their first and second meeting. These were the dreams that haunted him at night, no matter how hard he'd tried to fight them.

He leaned in closer, breathing in the scent coming off her lips. Sweet, yet salty. Tempting.

"Kiss me already," she whispered against his lips.

So he did. Gently at first, then when her lips parted, he tasted her more passionately.

She wrapped her arms around his neck, and pulled him against her. It was only now that he realized that despite her petite frame, she really was rather strong for her size.

She tasted of a gentle summer breeze. Fresh, refreshing even, with a hint of sweetness.

Her body felt cold against his, but not unpleasantly so. He cradled her in his arms, marveling at just how small and fragile she seemed to be. But every movement of hers reminded him that she was nothing of the sort.

She might not be a soldier like those of her kin he'd met in battle before, but she was a warrior at heart.

He could respect that, even admire it.

No matter what Broc was planning, Teaq could never settle for a human mate. He'd already known so before, but this first kiss only served to make him more determined. Islander women were strong and fierce as well, but they weren't *her*.

He hadn't been able to confess it to her earlier, but it was clear as day now.

There was only one woman that could make him weak. Her name was Liliwen, and she was in his arms right now. In a simpler world, he'd stay in this cave with her forever. He wouldn't just kiss her lips, but explore her body all over with his mouth. He would do so much more; unspoken things which only husband and wife did with one another.

But there was nothing simple about this world.

Teaq pulled back and studied Liliwen's face.

"What are you doing here with me, when it could get you into so much trouble back home?"

She smiled briefly, as she continued to hang onto him with both her arms crossed behind his neck. "Finding happiness."

How she could be innocent and sweet and fierce and brave all at once, Teaq had no idea.

She was an enigma.

"I was actually found out. Almost," she said, her expression turning serious.

The sudden change in her woke Teaq's protective instincts. "What happened?"

"The Seer, he said something that sounded a lot like me. He was looking right at me as well. I had such a fright."

Teaq shook his head. None of what she had said had made any sense. "What Seer? Said what?"

"Oh, we had our Premonition Ceremony last night. It was the summer solstice, you know," she said.

Teaq didn't understand that either, but didn't ask further questions.

"So when the Seer performed the ceremony, he said that a stranger was coming to the Black Isles which would turn everyone against one another. Brother against brother. Soldier against soldier. That the Isles would be at their weakest yet. The way he'd said it, I thought he was talking about me!"

Teaq's heartbeat sped up again. He didn't much believe in premonitions, but for the Sea Folk to hold a whole ceremony dedicated to it every year... Perhaps their Seer had visionary powers that the Islanders had no access to?

"And he wasn't. Talking about you, I mean?" Teaq asked, still concerned for Liliwen's safety, as much as his own.

She shook her head. "I shouldn't be telling you all this, obviously. But if my people do decide to attack... I don't want you unprepared. I don't want you in danger," she whispered.

Teaq nodded. He wasn't sure what he would have done in her place. His responsibilities to the Isles had always been the only thing he cared about. But with *her* in the picture… His own loyalties were well and truly challenged. It made sense that hers were too.

"So the Seer said that this stranger was human. With great powers."

Teaq's heart skipped another beat. Human. There was only one human the Seer could have been talking about. Broc's intended. And she was already here.

"You're sure he said it's a human?" Teaq asked. But in his heart he already knew the answer. That was why he'd been getting an off feeling about the whole situation.

Those were his instincts trying to tell him something. The human, Kelly, meant trouble.

He had to talk to Rhea. He could play on her jealousy to get her to be vigilant. If anyone could handle a powerful opponent, it was Rhea, anyway. Being a woman, she could get closer to Kelly than Teaq ever could.

Without tipping off his brother.

And if he could somehow convince Broc to be more vigilant as well…

"You look troubled," Liliwen said, as she snuggled her face against his chest.

The sweet girl had no idea.

"Thank you for telling me. You've helped me greatly."

"You're welcome," she whispered. "I aim to please."

Oh, if she kept on saying things like that, Teaq would find it impossible to keep things decent between them. Already his inner beast was screaming for her; desperate to claim her as his own.

She deserved better than this, though. She didn't deserve to be violated in a damp cave up on a hill on the Eastern Isle. She ought to be treated like a queen.

But instead, there was a treacherous human in one of the finest rooms on Black Mountain, scheming, plotting to bring them all down.

He kissed the top of Liliwen's head, marveling at how silky her hair felt. His own was crude and rough in comparison. She was something else entirely.

"Are you comfortable here? Not too dry?" he asked.

"It's perfect."

Teaq knew he had to get back to Black Mountain and speak with Rhea urgently, but he owed it to Liliwen to stay here with her at least a while longer. He owed it to his inner beast also.

And so he remained there, leaning against the mossy wall of the cave, with Liliwen in his arms. Sharing more kisses, caresses, and conversation.

He asked her about her home. What she got up to when she wasn't swimming across the Northern Sea, breaking the rules. She asked him about his achievements in battle.

It was perfect, just like she'd said. Until a good long while later, her demeanor seemed to change a little.

"What's wrong?" he asked.

"I'm okay," she said. The strain in her voice suggested she wasn't, though.

"No, really."

"It's just… a bit dry." Liliwen leaned back and looked at Teaq with large apologetic eyes. "I would have liked to stay a little longer."

Teaq smiled at her. "Come, let's get you back into the water."

Liliwen nodded, with disappointment written all over her face.

"Now, don't be sad. This isn't the last time we'll see each other." Teaq tried to sound upbeat to cheer her up, even if deep down he didn't want this moment to end either.

"Promise?" she asked.

Teaq nodded, and sealed his promise with a kiss.

———◆———

Back at the castle, it didn't take long for Teaq to find Rhea.

"We must talk," he said.

Rhea nodded darkly. "Our King hasn't heeded my advice."

Obviously the human, and Broc's instant infatuation with her, was the only thing on Rhea's mind these days.

Good. At least he wouldn't have to steer the coming conversation.

"I think we need to tighten up our surveillance on the human," Teaq said. "There's something I don't trust about her."

"Why, has she done something? Because if she has, you must tell your brother!" Rhea urged.

Teaq shook his head. "Nothing concrete, sadly. Call it instinct."

Rhea scoffed. "I've had that instinct from the very start of this whole mess."

"Indeed you have. I trust that in time we'll find proof that even my brother cannot overlook."

Rhea nodded. "How about we approach the Elders? If they look hard enough, they might be able to find something in the old scriptures that could help our cause?"

Teaq thought for a moment. The Elders had a habit of taking any suggestion and twisting it to their own objectives; or perhaps they were just so old that they merely forgot what they were looking for once they started reading. Still, it was the most innocuous way of getting ahead at this point.

"Fine. I will speak with Uri in confidence. Meanwhile, you keep an eye on her yourself."

"How am I supposed to do that?" Rhea complained.

"You're a woman, so you're allowed in her quarters. Find a reason to spend time with the human. Show her around the island for all I care. Or better yet, give her some combat training."

"Okay…" Rhea thought for a moment. "I suppose I can work with that. I'll plan something first thing in the morning. If the human can drag herself out of bed on time."

"Good. I'll find Uri now. We'll convene a Council Meeting once we have something to tell Broc."

Teaq left Rhea in the hallway he'd found her, and made his way straight to the Library, where the Elders spent most of their days. If now he could get Uri on his side, he might be able to act on the information Liliwen had given him without attracting any suspicions himself. He couldn't very well go around telling people he suspected the human because a Mermaid had shared some secrets from her own people. A prediction made by a mystic, no less.

Not only would nobody believe it, Teaq would soon find himself locked up for questioning himself.

And then not only would Kelly be beyond reproach, the entire defense of the Black Isles would be in shambles, just at a time when the Sea Folk planned a large scale invasion.

Teaq barged straight into the library, and found that Uri was sitting by himself at the large study table in the center of it.

He looked up. "Fancy seeing you here, commander. Planning to do some light reading?"

"Uri, I need your help," Teaq said.

Uri's expression turned serious. "Very well. There is something I have been meaning to discuss with you anyway."

Teaq's curiosity was piqued instantly. "What's that?"

"I've been studying these scriptures and I found a passage that concerns me." Uri pointed down at the tattered old scroll in front of him.

Teaq leaned over and was speechless as he read the words Uri had pointed out.

During a time of great change,
Two moons before the summer solstice,
A stranger arrives,
Hiding a terrible secret.
A power that could win or lose wars,
One that could destroy all or be our salvation,
Bringing with it the third great age of war,
As our enemies aim to acquire it for their own gain.

"Serendipity," Teaq whispered.

"Sorry?" Uri cupped his hand behind his ear.

"Thank you for bringing this to me, Uri. We must inform Broc immediately."

"What of the Reaping Feast? It's about to begin," Uri argued.

Teaq muttered a few choice words under his breath. The bloody Reaping Feast was becoming the bane of his life. "Fine. First thing tomorrow, then."

Teaq had never been superstitious. Until now he'd often wondered if the random stuff the Elders found in these old writings was 99% nonsense and only 1% useful. But tonight, his mind was changed.

In a twist of fate, everything had worked out exactly in Teaq's favor. Rhea would take Kelly out to keep an eye on her in the morning, and in the meanwhile Teaq and Uri would brief Broc with this latest bit of information. A concrete lead to start being a bit more careful with the human.

Teaq headed for the Great Hall with a spring in his step. Now, he would be unstoppable.

CHAPTER NINE

———◆———

Just how it had happened, Liliwen wasn't quite sure. But while waiting idly for Teaq to arrive at their designated meeting place, she had found herself swimming off course. At first it had been the birds floating in the sky that caught her eye.

Then a school of fish weaving their way through the pointy rocks that dotted the coastline of the Eastern Isle.

Her heart was light, full of excitement at the prospect of seeing him again. The memory of their first kiss in that magical cave was still vivid in her mind. That, of course, was the reason she'd come back so soon. She wanted more.

He loved her too. She was sure of it. He hadn't said it in so many words, but the way he'd kissed her… Surely that meant something. The way they'd spoken, more intimately than before… It was obvious now. She'd even told Cara about it already.

Still filled with hope and an energy she hadn't felt before, Liliwen swam on. Her mind was filled with a mishmash of idle thoughts. Cara was to marry Cadfael; the looks they'd shared during the Premonition Ceremony were undeniable.

And Liliwen was in love with Teaq.

Further and further she swam, discovering new sights

at each turn, and reliving old memories all at the same time.

Until suddenly, she could go no further. Something constricted her movements, and within moments, a frenzy of activity descended upon her helpless form.

All the excitement, all the joy Liliwen had felt just moments ago vanished.

She'd been caught in a net. And to make matters worse, the net had closed around her and she was being dragged to shore against her will. No matter how hard she fought, it was no use.

When she broke through the surface of the water, she saw not the familiar face she had been waiting for, but a whole lot of new people. Her heart grew heavy as she realized that the worst had happened. The Others had captured her.

Two of them were hauling her onto dry land.

"What is it?" Teaq called out in the distance, filling Liliwen briefly with hope again. Would he rescue her?

Her heart sank when she realized the truth that was written all over his face. The horror. He couldn't acknowledge her; no way.

If she said anything to suggest she knew him, it would only escalate things. For the both of them.

Struggling also seemed to make matters worse. The net was rough, painfully so. It rubbed her skin raw almost to the point of causing real damage. That was nothing compared to what these soldiers would do to her later, though.

"Well, let's see it," another man shouted.

Liliwen was quickly overpowered by the two men who had previously hauled in the net. One had wrapped his arm around her neck to keep her still, while the other took yet more of the hideous rough material from the netting and tied it around her wrists. It stung and burned against her skin, but she didn't let her discomfort show.

Instead, she took a moment to size up her captors.

The two soldiers looked rather unimpressive. One was a wolf, like Teaq, but actually he was nothing like Teaq at all. The other was something else, a bigger, furrier sort of creature. A bear, probably. Two more stood by a little further up the wall, with yet more of them overlooking the entire spectacle from the highest point of the fortifications.

Liliwen could barely stand to look at Teaq anymore, whose expression was one of pure horror, so she quickly skipped past him and looked at his companion. This man had the same animal form as one of the foot soldiers holding her, but he was more sizeable and wore fancier attire.

"Well, you don't see that every day," the stranger beside Teaq said.

From his armor, as well as the tone in which he addressed the others, Liliwen could make out that he was in charge.

"There's your intruder," the same man said, while

turning to face Teaq, who continued to stare at Liliwen. "Seems like the Elders might have been onto something with all their talk of prophecies."

Liliwen frowned. *Intruder,* that obviously referred to her, but what Elders? *What prophecies?*

The soldiers meanwhile tried to drag her up the stone steps to reach the wall level where the others were waiting. Liliwen wasn't sure how to react to all these strangers manhandling her, so she followed her instincts and spat at one of them.

This only enraged him further and earned her a firm hand to the throat.

"Don't lay a hand on me, wolf!" she threatened. Her anger had made her legs come out again, allowing her to stand strong on two feet.

Just exactly what she would do if he didn't let go, she wasn't sure of. But this wasn't a situation she'd ever found herself in, obviously. And the treatment she was receiving so far was unbecoming of how a princess of the Deep deserved to be treated.

If they knew her true identity, matters would undoubtedly get worse, though, so she stopped herself from berating them on royal etiquette and decided to cooperate. For now.

Just for a second, she dared to look into Teaq's eyes again. There was nothing but sadness there.

She couldn't let that affect her, though. She had to be

calm and calculating.

This romance of theirs had been doomed from the start. Just a fantasy.

But this right here, this was the cold, hard reality.

The worst had happened.

It had been a risk from the first moment she'd slipped out of her father's palace and come to these Isles. She had evaded it all this time simply because it was Teaq who had found her initially. And against all odds, they had connected. They had even fallen in love.

Now, all that was over.

She wouldn't be able to charm her way out of this situation.

Princess or not, she was a prisoner of war now.

"Lock her up underneath the deck so she doesn't dry out, then transfer her to a nice, cozy puddle in the castle dungeons at the earliest," the man in charge ordered.

Teaq didn't say a word.

"Brother?" the man spoke up again. "Will you accompany the prisoner transport?"

That last statement activated Teaq, whose one sentence response summed up the entire situation much more succinctly than Liliwen would have been able to.

"Dark days are upon us."

Indeed, they were. *Brother.* Teaq and the other man were siblings. The similarities were there, clear as day. Still, this revelation shocked Liliwen to her core. And although Teaq didn't show it right now, he looked to be higher up in the hierarchy as well. He wasn't just an ordinary soldier, but a commander, much like Cadfael.

Right now, he didn't look in charge of much, least of all himself.

Liliwen wished she could have a moment with him. To tell him that it was alright. That she was ready.

She was a prisoner, to be taken away and locked in the enemy's dungeon. She had known about this risk from the start and taken it anyway, just to steal a few more moments with Teaq.

Now, she would die for her indiscretions.

And once her father and Cadfael found her missing, and got Cara to spill all her secrets, all these people would probably die as well. Her family's vengeance would be swift as well as cruel.

And for what? For a choice she had made. A stupid decision, which had led her here again and again. She didn't even regret any of it, except to see Teaq so distraught. To know that her recklessness had hurt him, and would hurt so many of his people as well.

But she didn't get a moment with him and she could tell him nothing.

She was hauled across the wall, towards a large wooden vessel, where she was roughly deposited in the lowermost compartment, along with the same two guards who were meant to keep an eye on her.

As disorienting as it was, travelling like this, she still

knew roughly where she was. Her sense of direction was still strong. She closed her eyes for the duration of the boat ride, keeping track of each minute change of course.

If she managed to escape, it wouldn't be a problem to find her way home.

Of course, these people had no intention of letting her go, so these were just idle dreams.

She curled up on the floor, and rested her head on a pile of rope and just lay there, staring at the two dark outlines of the soldiers guarding her. The entire ordeal was a shock to her senses. She had been out of the water for all of one hour in her entire life, when she had spent those precious moments with Teaq in the cave only a couple of days ago. This was going to be a lot longer than just an hour. Staying on dry land for long wasn't just going to be unpleasant, it was also potentially dangerous for her.

Teaq's brother's order to prepare a puddle for her in the dungeons had sounded patronizing, but now she was yearning for even just a sip of water to soothe her burning skin.

She hoped beyond hope that they would show her this little kindness, even though she was their enemy, technically. And if not, she hoped that her end would be swift.

The boat rocked back and forth in the choppy waters of the Northern Sea. It was an odd movement, which threatened to turn her stomach upside-down.

Thankfully the journey didn't take too long.

Unfortunately it ended with her in a prickly sack of sorts, being hauled unceremoniously to her final destination.

Before long, she found herself deposited in a cold, damp room. The so-called dungeon.

There wasn't much light. Neither was there much water, much to Liliwen's chagrin.

The soldiers who accompanied her said their goodbyes by spitting on her, and slamming the door shut behind them. Finally, she was alone.

As desperate as her situation was, Liliwen couldn't stop thinking about Teaq. Where was he, and what was he doing?

Would she ever see him again? Or would he deny their connection and avoid her until she was eventually put to death. Part of her hoped that he would. She didn't want him to see her this way, covered in mud and filth, withered and mistreated.

It was unbecoming of her position. She didn't want to be remembered this way.

No, it would be best if he steered clear and never came down into this forsaken place.

Soon enough, it would all be over. She'd be dead and he might get on with his life.

Strange, these thoughts whizzing around in her head. How calmly she considered the benefits of her own demise. This was why her people were such formidable fighters. She'd never thought about it before, even during her lengthy conversations with Teaq.

It wasn't that Merfolk didn't consider their own mortality. They did. It was just that they—herself included—did so with a rationale that left little room for emotions and despair.

Death wasn't something to be feared.

After all, everyone was born, and everyone must eventually die.

Liliwen was ready to accept that her time had come.

CHAPTER TEN

he entire spectacle was horrific. Teaq could barely watch. None of the gore and violence of war could compare to the moment when his very own underlings hauled his Liliwen out of the water and took her prisoner.

She'd fought back initially, and valiantly so. But she was outnumbered, so it was a lost cause from the start. He had known that she was feisty and impulsive, so he half expected her to scream and shout at her captors, and call on him for help.

But she had done nothing of the sort. They had exchanged a couple of painful looks in silence, and that was that. She showed the sort of quiet resignation Sea Folk soldiers did in the rare occasions they were caught during battle. Like she had given up.

That was the most painful part, seeing the change in her. From defiant and proud to meek and helpless. As though her spirit was already broken, a mere ten minutes after her capture.

Teaq followed the patrol soldiers and Liliwen onto the longship. It felt as though they were taking *him* away with them as a prisoner as well. Or a part of him at least.

Just how she had ended up on this side of the island, and swam right into one of the islanders' nets, was unclear to him. She had been careless, but he could not blame her. She was not as worldly wise as she pretended to be. She did not know any better.

He should have protected her from all this.

Instead, he'd let her down. If only he'd scared her away after the first meeting. Or if he'd been clearer about which areas around these islands to stay away from.

Teaq had not been a stranger to disappointment in his life. Most notably when he lost the chance to become king to his little brother. That crushing defeat paled in comparison to what had happened today. Seeing Liliwen being hauled away in restraints was an image that would haunt him for the rest of his life.

So he remained silent for the entire journey back to Black Mountain, struggling with the ever present question: *how can I help Liliwen?*

He did not have an answer.

It was impossible not to lose hope.

Just what Broc planned to do with her, Teaq had no idea. But it couldn't be good. This was exactly the sort of thing they had been talking about. The next invasion was imminent. Liliwen would be branded a spy.

And Broc was convinced Liliwen was the outsider the Elders' prophecy had talked about.

But he did not know her; Teaq did. How could he possibly convince Broc that Liliwen wasn't a threat?

Meanwhile, there was the human to think about. The Sea Folk Seer had predicted that a human would cause a rift in the Black Isles that the Sea Folk could exploit. The Elders' prophecy had confirmed this, but hadn't pointed toward a human specifically, leaving Broc free to make his own interpretations.

Of course his little brother had been naive to consider the human innocent right from the start. And now that he'd seen her… It was obvious that he wasn't thinking with his head anymore.

Teaq had wanted nothing but to retreat to a quiet corner of the castle and drown his sorrows in ale, if that was what it took. But upon returning to the castle, he and his brother were intercepted by Rhea, who insisted that they follow her immediately. Broc was quick to agree, whereas Teaq was hesitant.

But the look Rhea shot in his direction left no room for wavering. Whatever she had to say, it was significant.

So they both joined her in the Great Hall, where she broke the news.

"As you're aware I have been taking the human out for combat training," Rhea started.

She talked faster than normal, as though she was agitated. Or excited. It was hard to tell.

"In the midst of showing her some moves with the practice swords, we were engulfed in a blue light. The human, she curled up into a ball, and I was thrown right across the edge of the plateau."

Teaq frowned. This wasn't what he had expected to hear. He glanced over at Broc, who didn't seem to understand a word Rhea had said to him so far.

"My king," Rhea spoke more firmly now. "The human, she's not what we thought. She cast a spell on me! If I hadn't been so quick on my feet, she might have killed me. I immediately placed her under arrest."

Broc shook his head, then started pacing back and forth through the hall. His footsteps echoed against the granite walls.

Teaq wasn't sure how to react either. Part of him felt like laughing, but he managed to keep himself in check. How bizarre.

At exactly the same time as his own world had fallen apart with Liliwen's capture, Broc's woman had been arrested by Rhea for performing witchcraft. It would be hilarious, if it wasn't so tragic.

Still, Teaq felt vindicated at having his suspicions confirmed. So far Broc had waved his concerns away as paranoia, but now... It was undeniable. The prediction Liliwen had shared with him had come true, as had the prophecy of the Elders.

"I don't understand. Are you absolutely certain that's what you saw, Rhea?" Broc asked.

"I would never lie to you, my king. She's a witch." Rhea put her hands to her hips in a show of confidence. She never did like her authority being questioned.

"It's really quite obvious that the prophecy is being fulfilled." Teaq tried very hard not to sound flippant, which he almost failed at. "We can only hope it's not too late to counter this attack!"

His remark earned him a furious look from Broc.

"This certainly demands further investigation, so we can determine what exactly has happened," Broc said. "And in case you've forgotten, we've just witnessed another incident that could very well be a part of this prophecy of yours."

That hit Teaq right where it hurt.

"It's quite clear what has happened, brother!" Teaq argued. "The witch felt cornered, out there doing combat training with Rhea, and she exposed herself for what she is. An infiltrator. An enemy disguised as an innocent peasant girl from West Hythe. Quite how the humans managed to find a witch after all these years, I cannot say. But she's here, so the hows and whys of it are irrelevant. This Reaping was obviously a trap."

"Now, now…" Broc raised his hand in protest. "We do not know for sure what the humans intended. Or if they even knew about this. After all, the prophecy speaks of a *secret* power. Perhaps it was a secret to them as well."

Unbelievable. Teaq was shocked at his brother's reaction. First he had refused to believe Rhea's account of events, and now he was arguing in favor of the mainlanders? What had gotten into him?

Rhea scoffed. "Fine, even if it was all *her* idea and *her* plan, and the humans had no knowledge of it. We are still at the brink of war. The prophecy—"

Broc slammed his fist into one of the tables lining the Great Hall, sending echoes across the room and making both Rhea and Teaq flinch.

"I am fed up of everyone's speculations! Sick of it! We *are* at the brink of war, but with the Sea Folk, not with the humans. We'll get to the bottom of this matter with Kelly also, of course. I will speak with her. I must—"

That sent Teaq over the edge. If he didn't control his anger, he would be tempted to plant a great big fist right into Broc's face.

"You will do nothing of the sort!" Teaq hollered.

Broc immediately swung around and adopted a threatening pose. "In case you have forgotten. I am King. I do not need your permission to—"

"My king, if you'll hear us out…" Rhea tried to defuse the situation.

Neither of the two brothers paid much attention to her.

"We do not know for sure if Kelly means us any harm. But we are *certain* that the Sea Folk are our most pressing enemy. Am I wrong?" Broc asked.

Teaq took a step away from his brother and tried to calm his breathing. His inner beast was a hair's breadth away from clawing his way out and showing his little brother just what he thought.

He was seething. And the worst part was, Broc's

assessment did make a tiny bit of sense. The Sea Folk were the confirmed enemy. And an invasion was imminent.

"I am going to interrogate our human prisoner now. Personally," Broc concluded.

No way! Teaq turned to face him again, but Rhea had already approached Broc.

"My king, I do not think it safe for you to see her unguarded. We do not know enough of her powers," she argued.

"That's enough! She's chained up. She even let you carry her down the hillside without attempting to fight back or escape. What is she going to do to me? Blind me with a flash of light?" Broc barked.

That was enough of that. Teaq could stand it no longer. He turned and marched straight toward the nearest door.

"Brother."

Broc's voice stopped him in his tracks, though he did not turn around.

"Perhaps you could interrogate the other prisoner. Find out what she knows and whom she's told. And for all our sakes, try to find out if her people are planning an attack."

Broc's suggestion got Teaq's mind working overtime.

Interrogate Liliwen. Of course ... As long as nobody knew the truth, he could come and go from her cell as much as he wanted. He could make sure she was well taken care of. That she was fed. Make the entire ordeal just a little less terrifying for her.

"She's not going to just spill everything," Rhea complained in the background. Oh, if only she knew the truth. Liliwen had already told him so much, without asking for anything in return. And all it had earned her was to be chained up and thrown in a dark hole underneath the castle.

"Use your powers of persuasion, brother. Our safety may depend on it," Broc said.

Teaq didn't need any more encouragement. Whatever Broc had meant by 'powers of persuasion', Teaq wasn't sure. But he wouldn't need any tricks to get her to talk.

He would head straight down to her cell and see her. But first, he would make a stop to pick up some food and some water along the way.

CHAPTER ELEVEN

Seconds merged into seconds, minutes into minutes and hours into hours.

Liliwen didn't know if day had turned into night, or even back into day yet. How long she had been locked up here, she had no idea.

No doubt Cara had noticed that she hadn't come home. Had her father found out yet? What about Cadfael?

What would they do once they did find out? Would her father, in a fit of blind rage at her disobedience, and encouraged by the Seer's predictions, order a large scale attack on the Black Isles?

She hoped she would never find out.

If she was in luck, she would be put to death before that.

Her skin was getting very dry; it was starting to ache more and more. Perhaps that was their plan. To leave her here to rot, until she dried up entirely.

It wasn't a nice prospect. A slow, painful death.

They hadn't given her any food either. Would she starve first or dry out?

Footsteps could be heard outside, which wasn't that unusual. There had been a guard outside from the very start, who occasionally wandered back and forth, patrolling the hallway.

This time, the steps were accompanied by an imposing and familiar voice. Liliwen couldn't hear what was being said, but she was pretty sure Teaq was outside. Her heartbeat surged.

He had come for her.

Sure enough, the wooden door of her cell swung open, and her rescuer appeared.

Unsure of who was listening, Liliwen chose not to speak at first.

Teaq entered and pulled the door shut behind him.

Liliwen wrapped her arms around her legs and just looked up at him in silence. She was certain she looked like crap. This was not how she wished to be seen. But he held in his hands the much needed thing that her body was dying for.

A pitcher of water.

"I'm meant to be interrogating you," Teaq whispered as he kneeled beside her.

"Has the guard gone? Can he hear us?" she asked, while reaching for the pitcher.

She dipped her hand in and instantly noticed how her skin soaked up the moisture. Such sweet relief.

"I sent him away," Teaq said.

Liliwen poured little splashes of water over herself, soothing the worst of the aches caused by the net as well as the general dryness in the air that had been getting the better of her. Once she had emptied the jug and looked up, she found that Teaq had been observing her the whole time.

"Stop staring at me, you're making me nervous," she complained. Her objection was only partially meant in jest.

Although she was grateful for the relief the water had brought her, a large part of her still wished Teaq hadn't come. Seeing him made it so much more difficult to accept her fate.

The pain in his eyes that she'd seen earlier was still very much there. Every time she looked at him, it tore at her insides. That was an ache no amount of water could fix.

"I'm so sorry," Teaq whispered.

"Whatever for? You couldn't have done anything. I understand that."

"I shouldn't have let things get this far," he said.

"Don't say that. Don't you tell me that we shouldn't have met. Don't take that away from me too," she threatened.

Teaq pressed his lips together and nodded. "Fair enough."

"How long have I been in here for? I can't tell if it's been an hour or a century," she said.

"Not even an hour."

Liliwen sighed. At this rate, her incarceration would be a lot more difficult to manage than she thought. All the time spent alone in here had passed at a snail's pace. Perhaps it wasn't so bad that he had come. At least his visit offered some distraction.

"Now, what are you supposed to be interrogating me about?" she changed the topic.

Teaq handed her a bowl full of something soft and slimy which she did not recognize. "Have something to eat first."

Liliwen's stomach was growling, but she wasn't too sure about this supposed food he'd brought. "What is this meant to be?"

"Fisherman's pie," he said, as though it was the most normal thing in the world.

"You make pie out of fishermen?" Liliwen frowned, then held it up closer to her face and sniffed it. Perhaps it wasn't so bad.

Teaq burst out laughing. "Not fishermen. It's made with fish!"

His correction made her chuckle as well. "Okay. I suppose I can eat that."

It had been an unintentional joke, but it still lightened the mood significantly. As she started pecking at the food and found that it was indeed better than starving to death, their conversation continued a bit more smoothly.

"You're not the only prisoner down here, you know," Teaq said.

Liliwen looked up from her bowl with great interest. "Do tell. Did you capture any more Merfolk?"

"Not quite. Remember the prediction of your people's Seer that you shared with me? It came true, somewhat. We had a human join our ranks some days ago," Teaq said.

"And you've imprisoned it too?" Liliwen asked.

"Well, not quite. Let me start at the beginning," Teaq began. He then shared the whole story of Kelly, the human offering, the Reaping Ceremony which the Others held, and how his brother had chosen her as his queen.

Liliwen found herself engrossed in his tale, asking for occasional clarifications when she didn't understand something. The strange food, meanwhile, was starting to get cold.

"And so Rhea, our cousin, arrested her and locked her up in a different part of the dungeon. Now it remains to be seen if Broc accepts the truth…" Teaq concluded.

"Love is a strange thing," Liliwen observed.

"What makes you say that?" Teaq said. "I'm telling you the prediction has come true, and you're bringing love into it."

"It's obvious he loves her, though. Your brother. And now both of you have had their women locked up. It's so romantic, isn't it?" Liliwen said.

Teaq frowned. "I wouldn't call it romantic, exactly."

"You ignored our peoples' age old conflict for me. Broc wants to ignore the truth that his woman is a witch."

"That's different."

Liliwen shook her head. *No, it isn't.*

Teaq looked at her in silence for a moment. "Well, romantic or not. I'm not sure I can find a way out of this."

Liliwen shook her head again. "There is no way out of

this. This is the end. It's fine, though. We'll be fine. You cannot expect your brother to accept something you cannot accept yourself."

Again, he was quiet for a little while.

"I'd better go, before word spreads and people start to get suspicious. Remember, I can only bring you food and water for as long as nobody knows about us," Teaq spoke up again.

Liliwen nodded, though part of her was dreading that she'd soon be on her own again. "That's obvious. You be on your way. I'm alright down here. But…"

"Yes?"

"There's a part of the prophecy that hasn't happened yet. My people will soon find me missing. It's only a matter of time before—"

"They'll come for you," Teaq agreed. "We cannot fix everything in one day. It will take them a while to figure out where you went."

Liliwen had to agree. The whole thing was inevitable. Neither he nor she could do a thing about it.

"I'll see you," she said.

He leaned in for a kiss, but she refused. Not here. Not in this filth. "I can't. I hope you understand," she whispered as she averted her gaze.

"I'll come back in the morning." Teaq got up and gathered the pitcher and bowl he'd brought, then he left. It was a relief, as well as a disappointment.

Hopefully morning would come soon.

———◆———

Teaq's visits were regular as clockwork. They helped Liliwen break up her days and nights. And now that she was sufficiently hydrated, thanks to the regular supply of water Teaq had arranged for her, her stay in the dungeon had become just a little bit easier.

At least it wasn't painful anymore.

And the stories he continued to tell her, of Kelly, the human; Rhea, his cousin; and Broc, the king, kept her imagination occupied even when he wasn't around. They discussed the challenges that lay ahead. The impending invasion of her people, as well as its repercussions, was something she thought about a lot.

Two nights and days passed. The next time Teaq arrived in her cell he was in a particularly agitated mood. Of course the first thing on her mind was just that; had her people come?

"No, no, nothing like that," Teaq grumbled.

"Then?"

"My brother has freed the human," he said.

Liliwen's eyes widened. "I knew it," she whispered.

Teaq frowned at her, but didn't comment.

From the start, she had wondered if the king would accept Rhea's account of events and stand by as his chosen bride remained locked up. Perhaps love had prevailed, at least for those two.

"What happened? How did Rhea react?" Liliwen asked, eager to get the full story.

This snippet of news was the most exciting thing that had happened in three days. She'd never been much of a gossip before, but being stuck in a dark hole had a way of changing people.

Teaq scoffed. "My brother didn't consult anyone. He just freed her, and had her attend the final night of the feast. I had a taste of her witchcraft myself."

Liliwen noticed herself leaning forward in anticipation for further details. "She performed magic? Right there at the feast?"

Teaq nodded. "She can read minds. Her talents are crude at best, though. I don't know how she managed to overpower Rhea on the hill top initially. She's one of the best fighters on the island."

Liliwen nodded slowly. This Rhea sounded very impressive from the stories Teaq had told so far. A woman after her own heart, not limited by the stupid rules the Merfolk had. Oh, to witness the confrontation between Rhea and the human, Kelly. Liliwen would have loved to have been there.

Teaq's stories had to suffice, though.

"So she read your mind?" Liliwen asked.

Teaq shrugged. "She tried. I heard her voice in my head. She was pleading with me to let her in, but she didn't seem to be successful. Rhea, though. She had Rhea eating out of her hand. It was a sight to see."

Liliwen cocked her head to the side. Indeed, it would have been.

"Did she tell you what happened? Rhea, I mean?"

"She was too shocked to say a word. I could see it in her eyes, though. The human had penetrated her thoughts. An entire conversation went on in silence. And by the end, Rhea was defeated."

"Wow. So the Seer was right. This human does have a power my people might fight over."

"I don't see how." Teaq's expression was still dark.

"Think about it. To see into the minds of your enemy. It's a valuable weapon to have."

Teaq was about to protest.

"Even if it doesn't properly work on everyone. Perhaps she's still learning to use her magic," Liliwen continued.

"Perhaps," he grumbled. "But for my brother to set aside everyone's opinions and free her on a whim… We're family. That should mean something."

Liliwen smiled briefly. How could this man be so stubborn? In the face of everything he was doing down here with her?

"Wouldn't you?" she asked coyly.

"Wouldn't I, what?"

"Wouldn't you free me, if you could?"

Her question remained unanswered, but the look in Teaq's eyes told her everything she needed to know.

CHAPTER TWELVE

O ne hundred and sixty seven hours. That was how long it had taken for Liliwen's people to track her down and launch their attack.

Teaq happened to be on the View Point when the war horn blew, rocking the castle down to its very foundations. It was a chilling sound.

All the more so because it was all his fault. His people would risk their lives in combat with the Sea Folk, because he had been stupid enough to enter into a relationship with one of theirs. Sure, technically it was her capture that had attracted King Weiland's wrath, but in a way it was only a matter of time before her presence at the Eastern Isle was discovered.

He should have known better.

Teaq forced himself into action. With his hand already tightly gripping his sword, he sprinted down the steps and through the winding corridors of the castle until he reached the drawbridge, shouting orders to any guard he found along the way.

He had started this. And now, he would be there at the frontline, next to his men, aiming to end it.

But what he found as he ran out of the castle and straight toward the fortified walls protecting Black Mountain's harbor, was just a little different than any normal Sea Folk invasion.

There were no hordes of angry soldiers, climbing out of the water and onto their island to confront his fighters.

That wasn't to say that there were no Sea Folk warriors in the water; there were hundreds, perhaps even a thousand of them.

But they were still submerged, just watching the islanders scramble into position.

In their midst, just out of range of the archers lining the castle turrets, was a floating vessel of some kind featuring a throne upon which was seated a Merman with the most impressive looking armor Teaq had ever seen. On his head, a crown of precious metals and stones; in his right hand, a long staff with three points on top. It looked like a ceremonial version of the spears Merfolk soldiers carried to battle.

Beside him stood another, younger Merman, who carried the usual combat gear of their people; a standard-issue long spear and a shield.

This was not an ordinary attack, otherwise the low ranking soldiers would have swarmed the island already.

Meanwhile, Broc was nowhere to be found.

Teaq scoffed to himself. Typical. Their world might be coming to an end, and his little brother was probably still in bed with his witch bride.

This made Teaq the highest ranking islander in present company, meaning that he would handle this however he saw fit. He filtered through the ranks of soldiers, reaching the front of the fortified wall and raised both his arms to attract the invaders' attention.

"I am Teaq, General of Black Isle's armies. I speak for my people. What is your business here?"

The figure on the throne stood up proud and arrogant as Teaq had come to expect from his kind. "I am King Weiland, protector of the Deep and rightful ruler of the Northern Sea. I have come to take back what's mine."

Teaq raised both his eyebrows, then quickly, before anyone got the wrong idea, turned to face his people. "Hold fire."

His order echoed through the ranks. Nobody moved a muscle.

Teaq turned back to face the Merking. "Feel free to clarify what you've come here to take."

As soon as he'd finished his sentence, he was joined by a disheveled looking Broc by his side.

"What have we got here," Broc asked.

Teaq gestured at the sea shell clad float in front of them. "King Weiland himself has graced us with his presence."

"First you will surrender my daughter, then you'll surrender these islands!" King Weiland bellowed.

Teaq was speechless.

"Did he just say his *daughter*?" Broc whispered. "Bloody hell, this is getting better and better."

Teaq was still frozen in place, when his brother stepped

up. "I am Broc Bearclaw, King of the Black Isles and Ruler of the Northern Sea. You'll have to take these islands from my cold, dead hands!"

"That can be arranged, you filthy land dweller!" King Weiland shouted back.

A rough prod in the shoulder brought Teaq back to reality. He exchanged a quick look with Broc. "I have to verify this. I mean, this changes everything."

Broc nodded. "Go. I'll handle this."

Teaq left his brother on the boundary and rushed back toward the castle. Although he didn't want to think of her this way, Liliwen, being the bloody Merking's daughter of all things, gave them leverage they previously did not have.

He had to speak with her, to figure out a way to resolve this mess while keeping bloodshed to an absolute minimum. The Sea Folk had arrived in great numbers. If they decided to strike now, there was no telling how long Teaq's men could defend Black Mountain. And if Black Mountain were to fall…

Teaq shook off these dark thoughts and focused on the task at hand. He had to see Liliwen. Immediately.

Although she was being held in a remote part of the dungeons, Teaq crossed the distance in no time at all. He ordered the guard away as usual, and quickly unlocked the door to her cell.

"We must talk," he said.

Liliwen looked up. "They're here, aren't they? I heard

the war horn. It shook the walls and ceiling. I thought the entire dungeon was going to fall on my head."

"Your father is here," Teaq said, folding his arms in front of his chest.

Her eyes widened. "He must be furious."

Teaq had wanted to be firm. After all, she hadn't been entirely honest with him. But seeing her cowering in the corner of her dirty little cell... He couldn't go through with it.

"He's furious with us for capturing you, yes."

"Oh. I..." Liliwen averted her gaze. "I didn't think he would come himself. He hardly leaves the palace."

"Why did you never mention you're a princess? King Weiland's daughter. Of course he's brought the full might of his army along with him to ensure your release."

"Perhaps for the same reason you never said you're your king's brother. And a general on top of it," Liliwen observed dryly.

Teaq couldn't suppress a smile. As usual, she had managed to cut through all the nonsense. "I think you'll find that I'm not merely *a* general, but rather the only general," Teaq corrected her.

"Fine. *The* general, and *the* princess. What does it matter, though? I'm still a prisoner and you're still under siege."

"They haven't actually attacked. Yet."

Liliwen looked up in surprise. "They haven't... That means..."

"He really wants you back in one piece, I suppose. That means we have all the leverage." It didn't feel right referring to her that way, but she had a practical way of looking at things so Teaq figured she would understand.

She nodded. "He wants me back so he can punish me himself. But yes, leverage."

"So what's left to decide is, do we attack first? What's the way out of this mess?" Teaq wasn't really asking her as much as he was thinking aloud. He was the military strategist after all.

"There's one thing…" Liliwen's voice had thinned to a whisper. "No, I couldn't ask you to do this."

"What is it? I'll do anything, as long as it helps," Teaq urged.

Liliwen's gaze met his, and he could see they were misted up. Ever since her capture, he'd felt close to tears at times, but not once had Liliwen shown this kind of weakness in front of him. Not once had she cracked under the pressure. It nearly broke him.

"Please, tell me."

"If you were to ask for a duel. Your strongest fighter against his." Her voice was cracking as she spoke.

Teaq frowned. This was her grand idea? "What good is that going to do?"

"You have to set the terms in advance. If he wants me, then you promise to set me free if his man wins. My father is many things but he's not dishonorable. He will respect the rules of a duel."

"So we will duel for you," Teaq mumbled, still trying to understand what she was trying to tell him.

"Well, you'll duel for whatever terms you set." Liliwen shrugged. "Demand a truce. Who's your strongest fighter?"

Teaq responded without hesitation. "Well, I am. That's why I hold the position of general."

Sure, Broc had beaten him in hand-to-hand combat seven years ago and won the throne, but that had been a fluke. Destiny, perhaps. Teaq had historically been the stronger fighter. Now, with the additional years of combat experience behind him, he was unchallenged. Undefeated in seven years.

"Who's your father's best fighter?" Teaq asked.

Tears had started running down Liliwen's cheeks. "Shh, it's alright. Have a little faith in me," Teaq whispered.

"I do. I do have faith. It's just… My father's best fighter is Cadfael. My brother." Liliwen turned away from Teaq and curled up into a ball, sobbing softly now.

Finally, Teaq understood. She had reluctantly offered him a way out. And she had foreseen this right from the start of their conversation. The other Merman on King Weiland's float must have been *him*. Liliwen's brother, Cadfael.

Sea Folk did not accept defeat easily. And because of what was at stake, neither would he.

He would fight her brother, possibly to the death. Two men she held dear, battling it out, all because of her. No wonder she was at her wits' end.

Teaq's heart had broken once, on that dark day of her capture. Now, it was threatening to shatter all over again.

"Don't cry. It'll be alright. Whatever happens." Teaq spoke these words because they were expected. But they sounded hollow.

Liliwen's sobs grew louder.

It was torture to stand there and watch as she broke down.

"Just go!" she shouted suddenly, startling Teaq.

He wasn't sure what to say.

"Go and get it over with! You don't have time for this. The enemy is already at your gate, readying for a fight," she cried.

Teaq nodded briefly. She was absolutely right, as always. The enemy *was* right outside. And he had a job, no, a duty to do. This wasn't just about Liliwen and him. It was about his people. About these islands, and everyone who lived on them.

First he would have to get Broc onboard with the idea, then they'd set the terms with King Weiland.

If he could win the duel, he could negotiate a truce for everyone.

"I love you," Teaq whispered, as he left her cell.

As he pulled the heavy wooden door shut behind him, he could still hear Liliwen's cries.

It took all his self-control to pull himself together and

not let his emotions get the better of him. His recklessness had caused all this. Now it was up to him to fix it.

It was time for him to face up to his mistakes and confess everything to Broc.

Teaq rushed back up the many stairs and across the drawbridge back to the spot where he'd left his men and Broc.

King Weiland was still waiting on his elaborate floating throne with Cadfael by his side.

Teaq took his own brother aside.

"I have confirmation." Teaq paused, then added: "And if I could have a moment alone, there's something else I have to tell you."

Broc frowned. "What, now? We're kind of in the middle of something here."

"Trust me. You need to hear this. Alone."

Broc nodded. "Fine. But make it quick. We have a war to fight."

CHAPTER THIRTEEN

The worst had happened. Beyond the initial shock, Liliwen hadn't cared about being imprisoned. She had accepted it. And Teaq's regular visits and stories about what was going on with Broc and the human had been a great help to pass the time.

But this… This was a horror she could not have foreseen.

She and her big mouth.

The two men she cared for. Her brother and her lover, standing on opposite sides of a battlefield. She knew how Cadfael fought. All or nothing. If he had half a chance, Teaq would not make it out alive.

Similarly, she knew Teaq would give his all in the duel. Either way, she would mourn a loved one's death by the end of today. All because of her stupid urge to go on an adventure. If only she'd stayed in the palace like her father had ordered her to…

Then she wouldn't have known this pain.

She wouldn't have known Teaq.

She would have never loved like she had loved him.

That in itself was something to regret as well. If she had known the outcome of her actions, would she have done it anyway?

Liliwen could do nothing but cry. Not for herself;

never for herself. But for the lives she had destroyed.

Cara. She had warned Liliwen. She had told her not to do anything stupid.

If Teaq won the duel... Liliwen would be solely responsible not just for the death of her brother, but her best friend's heartbreak as well. The guilt was overwhelming.

And if Teaq lost... Liliwen dared not think about how that would affect her.

The only thing left to keep her from losing her mind was that she was surrounded by these thick impenetrable walls. She didn't have to see it happen. She wouldn't even hear the fight.

Footsteps echoed down the corridor outside. Liliwen wiped the tears from her eyes and waited with bated breath.

It was impossible to gauge time down here, but that seemed too fast. Teaq couldn't possibly have come back already. Was her brother dead?

The heavy wooden door swung open yet again, only to reveal a stranger.

"Get up," he ordered.

Liliwen was frozen. What was happening? "Why, what's going on?"

"Look, I have my king's orders. That's all. Get up or I'll make you," the man spat.

Liliwen reached for a solid iron hook set into the granite wall of her cell and heaved herself up. She stood uneasily, but the guard didn't care. He dragged her around by her arm and tied her hands behind her back. Then he shoved her out the door and into the dark corridor.

"Where are you taking me?" she asked.

Had Teaq's brother decided against the duel and ordered her execution? Was this the end?

She stumbled through the maze of corridors, up multiple flights of stairs, with the guard continuously poking her in the back with the butt of his sword.

Her outburst from earlier had drained her, and the walk was long and strenuous. She blinked uneasily as she emerged from the final hallway, through a huge wooden drawbridge. Daylight.

The guard had taken her outside.

She could smell the salty sea air and feel the wind on her parched skin. A slow drizzle started, giving her body some much needed relief. Her mind was working overtime though. Why was she being dragged up here?

"There she is," the man she recognized as Teaq's brother, King of the Black Isles, called out loudly while pointing at her. "She's safe and sound, for now."

Liliwen blinked against the light, and finally saw who King Broc was talking to. Her father was waiting out at sea, seated on a replica of the throne he sat on at the palace, mounted on top of a floating wooden deck.

Liliwen's eyes filled with fresh tears as she spotted Cadfael standing beside their father's throne.

"Liliwen, have they treated you with the respect a princess of the Deep deserves?" King Weiland called out.

Through her tears, she nodded. "Yes Father, I'm fine." Liliwen's voice cracked a little as she spoke.

Of course, she was anything but. But the islanders' treatment of her had nothing to do with that. They didn't honestly plan to hold the duel here now, with her watching? She couldn't bear the thought. What a cruel and unusual punishment for her sins.

She looked around and saw Teaq, who was in the process of casting off his armor. So they had agreed on a simple duel, according to Merfolk customs. Only one weapon of choice; no shields or armor.

Whatever the outcome, it would be quick.

"The terms are set. The fighters are ready. Let the fight begin," King Weiland bellowed.

He gestured at Cadfael to make his way forward.

Teaq meanwhile ordered his soldiers back to clear a space on the fortified wall, just thirty or so feet away from Liliwen's current position. She was close enough to smell the blood.

And there was no doubt in her mind that there would be lots of it.

Teaq approached the makeshift arena. Mid-step, his human form warped and shifted. His skin sprouted fur, and his body elongated as she got down on all fours.

The sight took Liliwen's breath away.

For a moment, she forgot who she was watching, and

thought of all the stories Cadfael and the others had told of battles with the Others. Of the animal forms they had encountered and defeated.

Though Teaq wasn't carrying his sword anymore, he looked every bit the formidable opponent Liliwen thought he would be.

Similarly, Cadfael made his way toward dry land. His movements were smooth and powerful as he cut through the choppy waters. In one fluid jump, he emerged from the waves and landed on two feet onshore. The spectacle could not have been any more different from Liliwen's first steps on land.

Despite his smaller frame, Cadfael was imposing in his own right. Liliwen couldn't help but feel proud as well as afraid for both of them.

"Remember the rules," Broc, King of the Others, shouted. "My man wins, you forget you ever had a daughter and withdraw your troops immediately. Your man wins, we release her into your custody."

"What of the Isles?" King Weiland asked. "My man wins, you surrender the Black Isles along with my daughter."

Broc and Teaq exchanged a look. It was obvious that Broc was unhappy with the arrangement. But the prerequisite for a proper duel was that both parties agreed to the stakes in advance.

"Fine. Your man wins, you get your daughter as well as

the Black Isles," Broc said, then turned away in disgust.

Despite their differences, these two brothers, Teaq and Broc, must have had a great amount of trust in one another.

"Don't bloody lose," Broc hissed at Teaq, who nodded briefly.

Liliwen's chest tightened as the two fighters circled one another, waiting for the countdown. She didn't know who to root for, which side to take. Too much was at stake either way.

Whatever the outcome, the duel was already a tragedy.

The counting began, backwards from ten. Liliwen held her breath and turned away, only to be shoved back into position by the guard who had dragged her up here.

"You'll watch," he spat.

Liliwen pressed her lips together and fought further tears as the count hit zero.

Cadfael was the first to attack, leaping forward at Teaq with his spear raised high. Teaq dodged him effortlessly, then flipped back around and went for his arm.

But Cadfael fought him off easily and tried to slam the back of the spear into his head.

Another miss.

Teaq growled; the sound sent shivers down Liliwen's spine. Then he jumped up toward Cadfael, aiming right at his throat. Cadfael got down on his haunches, raising his spear up. It grazed Teaq's flank.

The Merfolk watching from the water cheered.

A sharp pain pierced Liliwen's heart, watching the spray of blood emerge from Teaq's wound.

But the injury did not slow him down. He recovered immediately and snapped at Cadfael's leg, taking a small chunk out of it.

Liliwen cried out in horror, then covered her mouth with both hands. The soldiers surrounding her on the fortifications roared in excitement.

Both fighters were now staining the ground with their blood as it dripped slowly but steadily into the dust. And both were completely unfazed by the pain. As if they didn't even notice it.

Evenly matched, they circled each other, attacking and defending in a deadly dance that lasted multiple rounds.

Neither showed any sign of slowing down, no matter how many times they were hit or scraped.

So far no serious injury had been inflicted, but it was only a matter of time.

Sure enough, it was Cadfael who succeeded first, slamming the long end of his spear into Teaq's ribs so hard Liliwen could hear the crack of bone.

Teaq fell and rolled over onto his side, before jumping up again and lunging at Cadfael with his teeth out. He bit down on Cadfael's right forearm, causing him to drop the spear. It clattered to the ground and was quickly pushed away by Teaq's paw.

The rules forbade any fighter from picking up a

weapon that was pushed out of the arena.

But Merfolk did not need spears to fight.

Even with a fractured arm, Cadfael's retaliation was quick. He punched Teaq in the side of his head, throwing him down and onto his back.

It only dazed him for a second, and Teaq was back on his feet and readying himself for another strike.

Both the fighters were limping now. Their skin and fur was getting covered in the same muddy red of the blood soaked ground. If one of them did not succumb to their injuries directly, blood loss would inevitably claim their strength.

Liliwen could bear it no longer.

"Stop," she whimpered. "Please, stop."

But nobody was listening.

The fight continued, on and on, until neither fighter had any unscathed body part left. Sweat, mud, blood and tears had mingled on their skin until they were barely recognizable anymore.

The fight was slowing proportionately to the amount of injuries either party had received. Their movements became clumsy, their dodges ineffective.

Would she mourn not one but both their lives tonight?

The ground was slick now. The water that lapped at the fortifications below was stained by the blood that had dripped down from the arena.

And still. Blow by blow, the two men continued to fight. Slowly. Badly. Giving it their last shred of strength.

Teaq, recovering from a blow to the rib cage, where Cadfael's spear had done its damage earlier, buckled at last.

"No!" she called out. *If you don't live, neither do I!*

Tears ran freely down Liliwen's face. She felt empty. Nothing left to give.

Four feet away, Liliwen's brother sunk to his knees, gasping for air. He looked up at her, mouthing just a single word.

"Sorry."

As both of them collapsed, so did Liliwen's world. A black cloud descended over her, pulling her down along with them. She did not remember anything after that.

CHAPTER FOURTEEN

Teaq tried to open his eyes, but could not see a thing. His lids were swollen shut.

He tried to move, but his limbs did not cooperate.

The pain coursing through his body was blindingly sharp, but that was not what he was most concerned about.

Liliwen!

The first thing on his mind was her. Windswept hair and cheeks streaked with tears. Broc had summoned her on King Weiland's demand. She'd seen the whole thing. How painful it must have been for her.

Where was she? More importantly, *how* was she? Was she safe?

He tried to open his mouth to speak, but his jaw was swollen shut. His throat was so dry, he could barely make a sound.

"Lili—" He coughed, then immediately regretted trying to speak at all. His chest was on fire, his mouth filled with the metallic taste of blood.

Of any of the battles he had been in, the duel had been in a league of its own. Lesser men might have given up sooner. But too much was at stake.

And the worst part was, he couldn't recall the outcome.

He was alive, wasn't he? Had he won? Had he

capitulated?

His head was throbbing so hard, he was certain that he was shaking along with it.

Where was he?

And where was everyone else?

What of his people? Had everyone been slaughtered by King Weiland's men, and he now found himself in hell?

Before he could try to speak again, he was pulled back under. Drowned in darkness, his mind gave way again.

———◆———

There were voices. Female as well as male.

And water. Waves lapped at her body, waking her gently.

Liliwen opened her eyes and could not recognize where she was. This wasn't her dark cell in the dungeon; rather, there was light all around, making it hard for her vision to focus.

Walls lined with shelves of colorful bottles. Her eyelids fell shut again.

Warm water surrounded her, coaxing her body as well as her mind back into reality.

"She's coming to," a female spoke.

"About bloody time," another responded.

Liliwen blinked a few times, and finally saw her present company.

There were two women, one with flowing red hair.

Short. Dressed in the most beautiful gown Liliwen had ever seen.

Another, much harder looking female, wearing an armored bodice, short skirt and not much else.

Kelly, the human newly crowned queen, and Rhea. Teaq had spoken about them so often during his visits to the dungeon, she was certain she recognized them.

Off to the side of the room stood Broc, looking in equal parts hesitant about being here, as well as concerned.

She looked down at herself and found that she was lying in a fancy basin filled with warm water. What was this place?

"Is she in decent shape?" he asked. "We don't want any more trouble."

What was she doing here? Why were they all talking about her as if she wasn't here herself?

"How is he?" she asked, though she was unable to articulate her question as well as she'd wanted to.

"What did she say?" the taller female, Rhea, asked.

"She asked 'how is he'," the human responded.

"Your brother will be fine. He's injured, but he will make it."

Liliwen choked back a sob. Her chest felt hollow, like someone had taken her heart and crushed it.

"She means Teaq," Kelly said.

"Oh."

Broc stepped forward. "Princess Liliwen. The challenge ended in a draw. Neither fighter could finish, so I've negotiated a compromise with your father, King Weiland."

Liliwen tried to process what he had said. *A draw? Did that mean…*

Teaq was still alive.

Again, tears flowed, but this time, they were tears of relief.

"You will be returned to your people as soon as King Weiland has ordered back his armies. This is how it must be."

Liliwen shook her head, then tried to raise herself out of the water, but slipped back down under. This tub was proving more effective in keeping her contained than any prison cell.

"I cannot go back," she protested.

"It's the only way. We break our word and your father invades. And with Teaq out of action, who will lead the troops?" Broc's voice trailed off.

"Will he make it?" she asked.

"Teaq? Oh yes, given a week or two, he'll be good as new."

Finally, some more good news.

But what would happen next? If the outcome of the duel required that she return to the Deep, then she had no choice but to comply.

Strangely, it had been easier for her to accept her fate as a prisoner. Having to return home and face her father… The humiliation would be immense.

And how would she face Cadfael, who had nearly given his life for her? And Cara, who had almost been widowed before ever being wed.

That wasn't even the worst part.

"Can I at least say goodbye?" Liliwen whispered.

Rhea scoffed, as did Broc.

"You seem to have forgotten that you and Teaq caused all this. He's my brother, and nearly gave his life to save these Isles, so I cannot judge him too harshly. But I have no love lost for you, Mermaid!" Broc said.

Liliwen averted her gaze. There was no arguing with his assessment. She was at fault. And now she had to face the consequences.

"I think she's well enough now. Even her color has changed back to normal," Rhea observed.

Liliwen raised her hands and looked at her skin. The warm water had undone all the damage caused by those endlessly long days spent in that dark cell. The only scars she carried now were invisible to anyone who wasn't a mind reader.

Liliwen eyed the human, Kelly, who had been silent during the final couple of exchanges.

So that was what a witch looked like. Had she already performed her magic and learned Liliwen's deepest, darkest secrets?

If she had, her expression did not let on.

"Then let's not waste any more time," Broc said. He turned around and left the room in a hurry. "Kelly, are you coming?" he called out from outside.

Kelly didn't move an inch, though. She kept on staring at Liliwen to the point of making her uncomfortable. *Please don't turn me into a fish or something,* Liliwen thought.

Kelly chuckled.

"What happened?" Rhea asked.

Kelly shook her head. "Just something I was thinking."

Liliwen cocked her head to the side. *You're listening right now, aren't you?*

Kelly turned around to check on Rhea, then made eye contact with Liliwen again and smiled briefly.

I understand, you know. The men ... they're finding it more difficult.

It was the strangest feeling, having this human—a creature Liliwen had never even seen before—infiltrating her mind like this.

Teaq told me your story. So romantic. From prisoner to queen.

What about your story? From princess to prisoner.

Liliwen shrugged. "Perhaps it is all written somewhere," she whispered.

Rhea turned to face the two of them "What?" She studied both their faces, then rolled her eyes. "Up to your usual tricks, I see. Well, I don't see what's keeping me here, then."

She still hates me. Kelly smiled apologetically, then turned and watched as Rhea left the room.

I'm sure she's not too fond of me either.

Will you be alright? You'll be released soon.

Liliwen lowered herself in the basin, wetting her hair. How good it felt to do that after so many days. *I'll have to be. Somehow.* It was still a scary prospect. Her father would be furious. She'd be monitored day and night.

You're not giving up on him, are you? Kelly raised her eyebrows in concern. *He loves you. I know he won't give up on you. I saw it in his thoughts during the fight.*

Alas, a glimmer of hope. Liliwen shook her head. No, she wouldn't give up.

Kelly nodded at her encouragingly. *Don't lose hope now.*
I won't.

They had only just finished their exchange, when Rhea returned, along with a number of guards. "That's enough of that, you two. It is time."

Liliwen bowed her head and surrendered as Rhea picked her up out of the slippery tub and set her down on the ground beside it. Her legs were shaking a bit, but she managed to stand on her own, briefly. Then the guards took her by the arms, and dragged her out of the room, through a maze of hallways, and finally, out of the castle. It all happened in such a blur, Liliwen could hardly find her bearings. Until she found herself in a familiar place, that was.

The fortified sea wall, where the duel had taken place.

Liliwen bit her lip hard as she spotted the makeshift arena. The ground was still soaked. The smell of stale blood hung in the air.

Broc, who had already been waiting by the very edge of the wall, cleared his throat. "So, as agreed. One princess, being returned hale and hearty to King Weiland. He would be wise to respect our deal."

Liliwen also hoped that he would. Even though she would not be able to stay in the Deep for long.

———•◆•———

The next time Teaq awoke, his eyelids opened just enough to let in the flicker of a torch some distance away. His surroundings remained a blur; nothing came into focus.

He did not recognize anything. Even his nose could not pick up any familiar scents. Perhaps he'd broken that too in the battle, along with almost everything else.

Every part of his body ached. But most of all, it was his heart that bothered him.

He had no idea how long he'd been out for.

And still he didn't know how the fight had turned out.

Where was Liliwen? Where was everyone else?

He fought the seething pain in his arms and chest and raised himself up. Now, he could get a better look at his surroundings, though his eyesight still hadn't cleared. He'd obviously received some significant hits to the head during the battle.

No problem, he'd heal. Islanders usually did.

But if Liliwen was still locked up somewhere, and there

was no one looking out for her, then she might not make it that long. He had to make himself noticed. He had to know what was going on.

Teaq inhaled deeply, only to cough violently. After catching his breath, he tried again.

"Hello?" he called out.

His voice sounded pathetic. Weak, just like the rest of him.

Another coughing fit forced him onto his back.

Footsteps approached. Thankfully, his efforts hadn't been in vain.

"Come quick, I think our general has come to," someone called out.

At least he was among his own people. That was a good sign.

More voices could be heard now, approaching his position.

Teaq tried to focus again, but he could not recognize the faces that surrounded him now.

"Sir, can we get anything for you? Water? Food?" someone asked.

Teaq shook his head. "Broc. Get the King."

"What did he say?" another person said.

"The King. He means to speak with King Broc."

"No problem, Sir. We will send someone to find him immediately."

Teaq closed his eyes and just tried to breathe deeply. Ideally he would not be talking right now. He should just surrender to the healing process. There was a reason fighters passed out, often for days, after a particularly rough battle. Islanders healed quickly, much quicker than humans or Sea Folk. But they could only do so while at rest.

The more he fought it, the bigger the risk of permanent damage.

But there was no way Teaq would allow himself to fall asleep again without finding out what had happened. He had to know if Liliwen was safe.

Footsteps could be heard moving back and forth. His attendants had dispersed again.

Perhaps they had more soldiers to look after. More casualties of battle.

Teaq didn't know how long he lay there, with his eyes closed, listening to the sounds in the rooms or halls surrounding him. Where was he, anyway?

He had almost given up, when at last, he heard a commanding voice in the vicinity. "Where is my brother? Take me to him!"

Teaq forced his eyes open just in time to see the outline of Broc's person standing in front of him. At last, he would find out the truth.

CHAPTER FIFTEEN

he swim back to the Deep was long and arduous. Not because she was physically struggling, but rather, because she dreaded it. Liliwen was accompanied by a handful of guards from the palace, not the sort of people one could have a proper conversation with.

No, she was basically on her own with her thoughts.

When the palace came into view, her heart sank even lower. She'd expected to be executed by the Others, but she'd never planned for this. Death would have been simpler. Less messy.

Liliwen and the guards had barely made it inside the strong walls, when she was almost assaulted by Cara.

"I told you! I told you not to go. Not to do anything stupid. And you had to go off anyway! How dare you!"

Liliwen froze.

Cara had obviously been crying. And why wouldn't she be? Liliwen's recklessness had affected everyone back home, especially Cara, who had no doubt been caring for an injured Cadfael since his return from the duel.

"Sorry," Liliwen whispered. "I'm so sorry."

Cara pressed her lips together and looked at her for a moment. It was the most awkward of silences. Liliwen did not know what to do with herself.

"Oh, Lili! I thought I'd never see you again!" Cara cried out at last.

Liliwen still didn't know whether to stay or run, when Cara wrapped both her arms around her and hugged her tightly.

Liliwen hid her face in her best friend's hair and her eyes filled with tears as well. This part, at least, had not gone so badly after all.

"How is he?" she asked. "How is Cadfael?"

Cara pulled back. "He fought bravely for you."

Guilt filled Liliwen's heart, threatening to overwhelm her all over again. He *had* fought bravely. Both of them had. Her two heroes. If only they knew she had been rooting for both teams.

"Come with me. We'll go see him."

The guards had stood by in silence so far, but now one of them made his presence known with a cough. "Princess Liliwen, we are to bring you to your father immediately."

Oh dear.

"In time. Allow her to see her brother at least, who came so close to giving his life to ensure her safety! It's the least you can do!" Cara argued.

The guards exchanged a few awkward looks.

"I'm afraid we must insist," the same one spoke again. "Orders, you see."

Time to face the music. Liliwen took Cara's hand and squeezed it.

"I'll come find you soon," she said.

Cara nodded. "You'd better."

Lord, give me strength.

—◆—

"**B**rother, you cannot be serious!" Broc complained.

Teaq just stared at him. He was. Deadly serious.

"You of all people ought to understand. Your own woman was a guest at our fine dungeons not so very long ago. After attacking one of our own, no less! And it took you all of two hours to get her released in secret."

"But… She's a Mermaid! She's the enemy! You've been harping on and on about the next invasion. Well, in case you forgot, it arrived already. To get *her* back!"

Teaq sighed. His head was pounding and he was fighting shooting pains in his chest, but this was a conversation he could not put off any longer. He'd had a lot of time to think while in recovery, and it was the only thing that made sense to him.

"Brother, she will not stay in the Deep. She will come back. And when she does, wouldn't it be wiser if I made sure she wasn't here for the Sea Folk to come and retrieve?"

That was the story Teaq told Broc, anyway. In truth, even if she did not come back, he was prepared to venture out there and find her for himself.

As he'd drifted around the edges of consciousness these past few days, she had been on his mind the whole time. He would not give her up so easily. Life wasn't worth living if it wasn't with his Liliwen.

"How can you be so sure? What if all this time she was a spy, and she was just toying with you. What if she's back home now, telling them all about our weaknesses, so their next attack will really hit us where it hurts?"

"How could you be so sure about Kelly?" Teaq retorted.

Broc paced the room, as he usually did when he was struggling with something.

There really was nothing more Teaq could say to convince him. He hadn't seen it that way at first, but Liliwen's comparisons between their own situation and what Broc and Kelly had gone through were starting to ring true now.

They were both slaves to their emotions. Nothing any outsider could say or do would get in between either couple.

Teaq and Liliwen were meant to be. Whether Broc chose to accept this fact or not.

"And what of your duties here?" Broc asked at last. "We need you. *I* need you here!"

That was the one weak spot in Teaq's plan. He didn't have a proper answer. But he knew he had given all he could to Broc and the Isles. Now it was time for Teaq to do something for himself.

"You could promote Rhea to general. She's been a formidable head of the Royal Guard. A fearsome fighter in her own right. She's proven herself worthy many times over," Teaq suggested.

Broc stopped pacing. "She's a good candidate. But I still don't like it."

"Have I ever asked you for anything before?" Teaq said. "Plus, you have an advantage over the Sea Folk now. One that we never had before. Kelly's powers will only grow as time goes on."

"Kelly," Broc mumbled. "As much as I'd hate to involve her in the ugly business of war, it may be inevitable going forward."

As painful as it was, letting down his little brother, he could not help it. From the moment Broc had taken the throne, this moment had been inevitable, whether either of them realized it or not. Sooner or later, their relationship would change again.

It was just ironic that it happened because of a woman. Teaq had never thought himself capable of changing his entire outlook in life for love.

But it was too late for second thoughts now.

"Then you know what to do. As do I," Teaq concluded.

"Her people will come for her. Again." Broc's expression darkened further.

"They will. But this time, you and Kelly will be ready."

"I hope so."

"And if not, there's always Saras…" Teaq said.

Broc looked up in horror. "No, I couldn't. He's been asleep for so long… Don't you remember the stories Father told us of what happened before he went to ground?"

Teaq nodded. "I remember. But between a witch and a dragon, there's no way the Sea Folk can compete with that."

Broc sighed. "There will be challenging times ahead."

Truer words had never been spoken.

"Where will you go, anyway?" Broc asked.

Teaq shrugged. "Wherever Liliwen's people won't find us."

"I hope you know what you're doing."

As do I. Teaq closed his eyes, giving them much needed relief. It would still be a few days before his body regained enough of its former strength to put his plan into action. Until then, he'd have a lot to think about.

"I'll see you, brother," Broc mumbled as he made his exit.

Teaq would have liked to be able to help. But Broc was king. In the end, the safety of these Isles was his responsibility.

———◆———

"You have returned." King Weiland's statement almost sounded like an accusation.

Liliwen kept her head bowed, careful not to make any move to enrage him. "Father, I apologize for all the trouble I have caused."

"Mhmm."

She waited, but there was deadly silence all around. It was enough to drive a person mad.

This couldn't be it. The hammer would drop any second now. Yet, minutes passed without a word being said between them.

Liliwen dared not move.

"I had ordered you to leave the fighting to Cadfael, had I not? Or had I just imagined that? Are my orders not good enough for you?" There it was.

"I'm sorry, Father. I did not mean-"

"Silence!" King Weiland roared.

Liliwen flinched.

"You will speak once I am finished! Do you understand me?"

She nodded.

"What was that?"

"Yes, Father."

"It seems you felt the rules do not apply to you, because you are my daughter. You'll address me as your king from now on. So you do not forget that my orders stand, regardless of what our relation is!"

"Yes, my king," Liliwen whispered.

Of course he was furious. She had ignored a direct order; something nobody else would have dared to do.

"I ought to lock you up and throw away the key. But it seems the Others beat me to it."

"Yes, my king. Punish me any way you see fit."

"How could you be so stupid? After the premonition ceremony promised us good fortune this season. We weren't ready. The element of surprise; ruined!"

"I am ashamed of my actions, my king."

"As you should be! You have set us back months, if not years. And your brother, he's been severely injured because of you!"

Liliwen's chest tightened. That was the worst part. She did not give two hoots about the invasion or the war effort. But people she loved had been hurt. All because of her.

"I wish to see him. To thank him for his courage," Liliwen mumbled.

King Weiland got up from his throne and towered over her. He was tall for a Merman, but not compared to the Others.

"You will see him, and you will beg him for his forgiveness."

"Yes, my king." She intended to.

"And once you do, you will return here at once, and await your punishment."

"Yes, my king. I deserve punishment."

With her head still hanging low, Liliwen slinked out of the coral hall, leaving her father alone with his anger.

If he wished to imprison her, fine. He couldn't keep her—his only daughter—locked up forever. She would bide her time, and make one final journey away from here.

After everything, this place no longer felt like home.

CHAPTER SIXTEEN

L iliwen turned around to face the guard who had been shadowing her since her return. "Where are they keeping Cadfael? Take me to him," she said.

The guard led the way as they crossed into the residential wing of the palace.

This part would be the most painful. The guard opened the door to the infirmary and showed her in. Liliwen held her breath as she stepped inside.

Nothing could have prepared her for the sight that awaited her. Cadfael, laid up on blood stained sheets. His wounds were still seeping, even though they had been covered in medicinal tinctures and seaweed. He was in bad shape.

Cara sat on a stool beside him, tending to his many bandages.

"Oh, Cadfael, I'm so sorry," Liliwen cried out as she approached.

He opened his eyes, and smiled awkwardly. His formerly handsome features were disfigured by bruises and cuts.

"What does the healer say?" Liliwen turned to ask Cara.

"It'll take time, but nothing permanent," Cara responded.

"I'm sorry I couldn't win for you," Cadfael said.

Liliwen burst into tears and buried her face in her hands. "Oh, brother. I have been so unfair to you. This is all my fault."

"Shhh, little sister. I'll be fine. It's a soldier's duty to fight for his princess after all."

Liliwen looked up through her tears. "I must tell you something which might change your mind."

"Yes?"

"The Other you fought… he…"

Cara gasped and covered her mouth. "It was *him*, wasn't it! I don't believe it."

Cadfael frowned as he looked first at Cara, then back at Liliwen. " *Him*? Him, who?"

"Brother, while you have been courting Cara, I'm afraid I had an ulterior motive to visit the Black Isles again and again too…"

"She's been hanging around one of them. One of the Others," Cara added. "I did not tell your father this, but…"

Cadfael closed his eyes and breathed in deeply. "Things are falling into place."

Liliwen sank onto the other chair beside Cadfael's bed and lowered her head into her hands. "I'm so sorry for everything. For putting you in harm's way. For dragging you into a fight you could not win," Liliwen said.

"Oh, I could have won!" Cadfael protested. "It was not a totally fair duel, though."

"How so?" Cara asked.

"I did not mention it to anyone, but when *he* entered the ring, he spoke to me. He said he wished not to kill me. For your sake. That he was fighting for your safety as well."

Liliwen looked up in shock. "He said what, now?"

"I did not know what to believe, but something in his tone gave me pause. I tried not to kill him either. Did I?"

Liliwen shook her head. "No, he's alive."

"Well then. Everyone got what they wanted. The Black Isles got a truce of sorts, and we got our princess back."

Liliwen's fragile heart could take it no longer. She had to confide in them fully. Her secrecy had brought everyone nothing but trouble. No more.

"I intend to go back."

"What? You cannot! As your best friend, I forbid it!" Cara exclaimed.

Liliwen got up and took her friend's hands. "Don't you understand? What you have here with Cadfael, I have with him. He walked into the duel knowing Cadfael would try to kill him, and yet he sought to spare his life for me. I love him, Cara. I cannot be without him."

Now it was Cara's turn to cry. Cadfael, meanwhile, was stoic as ever.

"I wish it could be any other way, but it can't," Liliwen added.

"Oh, Lili… I don't know what to say," Cara sobbed.

There was nothing she could have said. Liliwen had

made up her mind.

"Father will not be happy," Cadfael observed. "He'll break the truce in retaliation."

"Then I'll have to make sure I'm not on the Isles for him to find."

"Where will you go?" Cara asked.

Liliwen shrugged. "Far away. Beyond Father's reach."

Cadfael opened his eyes again and reached for Liliwen's hand. She closed her fingers around his. Despite his injuries, he still had a firm grip.

"Little sister, I hope you know what you're doing. And you're not walking into another trap."

"My heart is already with him. And a person cannot live without a heart."

Their moment was interrupted by the guard, who first knocked, then opened the door.

"My princess, it is time. Your father means to deliver his punishment."

Liliwen shared a long look first with Cadfael, and then Cara. "I'm so glad I could tell you both the truth."

"Be safe, little sister," Cadfael said.

"Be safe, brother."

As she returned to the coral hall, accompanied now not by one guard, but half a dozen of them, Liliwen felt like an offering being brought to slaughter. She wasn't sure what to expect, but when she saw the hooded soldier, already holding his whip at the ready, she realized that she hadn't expected *that*.

King Weiland looked on from his throne, not a word said between them.

The first crack of the whip shocked her in its harshness. Then, Liliwen braced herself and prepared to endure the rest.

Two good men were laid up with severe injuries because of her. It was only right that she received her fair share.

For Teaq, she told herself as the whip came down hard on her back again.

For Cadfael. Blood started to flow soon thereafter, as her skin gave way.

Four lashes done, seventeen left to go.

No longer would she possess flawlessly beautiful skin. After this, her sins would be etched into her back forever, for all to see.

When she looked up, after it was all done, she noticed that her father was no longer present. Just how long ago he had left, she did not know.

———◆———

"You came," Liliwen spoke first. Night had come and gone once since her arrival. Still, she hadn't moved an inch from her position to avoid detection and capture. She wouldn't make the same mistake again.

"Was there any doubt in your mind?" Teaq asked.

Liliwen shook her head. "And anyway, I would have

waited for you, for as long as it takes. Forever."

"I wouldn't have," Teaq said.

Liliwen's chest tightened. Although it had happened days ago, the lashes on her back still stung. A painful reminder of what she had endured, and would endure again for her transgressions. "You wouldn't have?"

"If I hadn't found you here, I would have sailed all the way to the Deep to get you."

Her heart softened and she smiled. "Just how exactly would you have done that? A one-man assault on the palace, without being able to breathe underwater?"

Teaq shrugged. "I would have found a way."

"Aha." Liliwen cocked her head to the side. "*Sailed* to the Deep, you say?"

"I have a vessel. It's moored not too far from here. It's small but seaworthy."

Liliwen followed Teaq's hand as he pointed at a wooden structure visible in the distance.

"We cannot stay here," Liliwen observed.

Teaq shook his head. "Indeed, we cannot. Your father—"

"He'll come looking for me again. This time he won't be content with a duel."

"We just have to decide where to go," Teaq said. "The mainland is not an option. The humans would kill either of us on sight. And if we go west, our route would lead us right to the Deep."

Liliwen breathed in deeply. She wanted to remember

this place in as much detail as possible. Where everything began.

"I know of a place," she said. "I mean, I've heard stories."

"Where?"

"It's off to the north-east. At the edge of the world. If it exists, we'll find it." Liliwen looked up at Teaq, studying his face. When she had left, Cadfael had still been covered in cuts and welts. Teaq looked in better condition, but there was still something off about him. "How are you doing? I heard you were badly injured."

He shrugged. "I'm fine enough. A few more scars to add to the collection."

Liliwen nodded. Her punishment had earned her a fair number of scars of her own.

She reached for Teaq, who took her hand and helped her out of the water. This time, she did not protest when he lifted her up in his strong arms, though his touch on her injured back made her whimper slightly.

He carried her across the pathway to his boat, and finally Liliwen felt like she could relax. She had left in the dead of night, from the infirmary where she was meant to recover from her punishment, straight into the vastness of the Northern Sea. Her journey was not yet over, but at least she did not have to go it alone anymore.

In Teaq's arms, she felt safe. Like nothing and no one could hurt her ever again.

But things had changed from the last time they'd met each other here.

They were no longer innocent. No longer carefree.

Both had suffered for their love.

Liliwen knew it would take time for them to find their way back to each other.

As she watched him prepare the sail and haul up the anchor of his boat, she had to smile despite everything.

It would take time, but now that they were together, sailing away into their new life. They would have nothing but time.

As the boat started to move, and Teaq set its course to northwest had Liliwen had said, they both stood side by side, watching the Eastern Isle get smaller as they moved further and further away from it.

Bye bye, Black Isles, Liliwen thought.

"It's strange. I'm leaving everything I've ever known," Teaq observed.

Liliwen turned to face him. She had to strain her neck to get a good look at his face, that was how tall he was. "I have everything I need to know right here," she said.

Teaq looked down at her and smiled.

She realized then that he hadn't changed at all. He'd been a battle-hardened soldier all along. That was part of his appeal.

She wrapped her arms around his neck, and he lifted her up again so their faces were at the same level.

"And I wouldn't have it any other way," she added.

"Me neither." He glanced back at the island for a moment, then looked at her again. "The course is set. As long as the winds don't change, there is nothing for me to do right now. What do you say we retreat below deck for a while?"

Liliwen's eyes widened as her heart started to beat a little faster. "I would like that very much."

Since the first time they'd met, right up to the time he took her up into that secluded cave, so many questions had been on her mind. So many fantasies left unexplored.

She would find her answers now that they were finally completely alone.

EPILOGUE

Teaq lay Liliwen down onto her back, admiring her beauty, which shone brightly despite the dim conditions below deck.

The simple cot was not fit for a princess.

None of this situation right now was as she deserved.

But in all its imperfection, this moment still felt completely right.

He kneeled beside the bed, fighting stiffness in his legs as he went down.

As she ran her hands up and down his aching body, all the pain started to melt away. He had not come out of this unscathed. The wounds would take time to fade. The fractured ribs, especially, would keep on bothering him for a while. That was fine, though. He was used to it.

But as he looked her up and down, he found that she also, had been changed. She was not as free in her movements, not as deliberate and in control as she had been previously.

She turned onto her side to make room for him, and he saw a glimpse of something different.

Her skin, which had previously been a flawless expanse of greenish flesh, had blemishes now. Red, and angry looking.

He leaned over to get a better look at her back. What he saw shook him to his core.

"My god, did my brother have you caned while you were locked up? Why didn't you tell me, I would have stopped it. I would have—"

"Shh," she said. "It's alright. Your brother did not do this."

He took her face gently into his hands. "No, it's not alright. I made a vow to myself to keep you from harm."

"It is the punishment my father chose. Considering what I put you through. And my brother, as well, it's only fair."

Teaq looked deeply into her eyes. They had both sacrificed. Fate demanded its pound of flesh from everyone, without exception.

He leaned in for the first kiss in ages. How parched his lips had been without feeling the softness of hers. How hungry was his flesh, now that they were free.

She responded instantly. The passion he'd felt earlier, when they had shared their first intimacies, was back with a vengeance. Their bodies were desperate, aching to become one.

Liliwen grabbed him by the back of his neck and guided him closer, onto the small bed with her. It barely fit them both, but it would suffice.

Through the grazes and cuts that still lingered on his skin, pain mixed with pleasure, until he could no longer distinguish one from the other. She seemed to feel the same.

The awkwardness from before vanished, and she took on a more active role with him.

Every touch of his, she answered with one of her own. Every exploration, she seemed to savor just as he did.

"You're so warm," she whispered.

Yes. Yes, he was. And she was not. Her cool skin was pleasantly soothing. Despite the fresh scarring on her back, her skin still had a smooth quality to it that he had not known before touching her.

It was addictive. Tempting. Seductive.

"We don't traditionally do this. Not without a formal union," Teaq said.

He wasn't sure what he meant by that, because he certainly did not intend to stop now.

"You mean, a wedding?"

"Yes." Teaq leaned down and kissed the dip underneath Liliwen's collarbone.

How beautiful she was. The greatest artist in the world could not have sculpted perfection like her.

"So marry me, then," she said.

Teaq pulled away from her to look her in the eyes. Golden, with a depth not unlike the seas they currently sailed on. The seas that were her home.

"There's a whole ceremony. It doesn't just happen."

"It doesn't just happen for us either. You'd have to ask my father for my hand. We both know that's not going to happen," Liliwen said. "But we're not like our people anymore. Perhaps we can make our own way."

Teaq smiled. "I like that. We'll do it our own way."

"So. What happens in your ceremony that we can do?" she asked.

Teaq thought for a moment, and looked down at the many items of jewelry that still adorned her gorgeous body. "We exchange rings."

She did not hesitate for a moment, and took off one of her rings and presented it to him.

"We have to say our vows first," Teaq said, while weighing the gold ring in his hand.

"Sure. How do they go?"

"I ought to know this, but then, I've never been married before," Teaq joked. This wasn't a joking matter, though. He'd never planned this for himself, but that didn't make it any less special or important.

He slipped off the bed and kneeled down again, with the ring in the palm of his outstretched hand. "With this ring, I promise to keep you safe, to love you and care for you, until death takes me."

Liliwen took the ring and placed it back on her finger. Then she removed another, as well as one of the multiple chains around her neck.

"With this ring, I promise to keep you safe, to love you and care for you, until death takes me." She leaned down and reached around his neck, fastening the chain on him.

He reached for it, feeling the little gold ring that hung from its lowest point.

"That was beautiful. The vows, they're so romantic," Liliwen swooned.

"I'm not sure those were the actual words," Teaq said.

She shook her head. "They are now. For us. I'll never forget them."

He wouldn't either.

Liliwen smiled and gestured at him to get back onto the bed. "Now nothing stands in our way. Neither tradition nor law."

"We're free to do as we like. Until death takes us."

"Until death takes us," Liliwen repeated after him.

She wrapped his arms around him again and coaxed him on top of her.

All this time he hadn't been sure how this part would work with her, and of course berated himself for thinking such crude thoughts about a woman so pure. He needn't have worried, though.

As more and more of his armor and clothing came off, to be discarded on the floor, their bodies knew exactly what to do. Instinct took over.

Liliwen's body had already adjusted to being on dry land; her transformation had become easier each time she had come out of the water.

Two legs, much like his own anatomically, which spread to reveal very human, or islander-like features. Her hands continued to explore him. His chest, with its chiseled muscles and bit of hair that she seemed utterly fascinated by.

His back and buttocks, along with the fresh scars that still occasionally stung. It was a sweet pain, one he could not get enough of so long as it had been caused by her touch.

Finally, her hand reached down, where his manhood was already standing proud. Her grip sent shivers down his entire body.

She was firm, with him. Self-assured, just like a lover should be.

Their love knew no shyness. No shame.

"I've been wondering what this would be like, right from the start."

She had said exactly what had been on his mind all along.

He reached down between her legs, and found that indeed there was one spot where she wasn't cool to the touch. She was red hot, and wet for him already.

"Ohhh, that feels so good," Liliwen moaned.

Her words were superfluous. Her entire body had told him already.

As her hands gripped him tighter, his inner beast was raring to get out and take over. His most base instincts were clawing their way to the surface.

"I'll pleasure you the way you deserve to be pleasured," Teaq spoke in a low growl. "My princess."

Liliwen moaned again; her voice was musical. It enchanted him, spurring him on to do better.

He positioned himself between her legs, and sought to enter her.

"Please me, my husband," she said.

That last statement sent him over the edge of control. He pushed his way into her, and felt her body close around him.

If this was somehow wrong, if it was against the rules, even against nature, their bodies had no idea. Everything about it felt absolutely right.

She bucked her hips upward, drawing him in closer.

He responded with a kiss to the side of her neck.

So beautiful. So fragile and yet so strong.

His wife. His Liliwen.

He thrust into her, again and again. Deeper and deeper. Her hands found their way to his hips, guiding his movements. They were in perfect harmony. Two bodies, one soul.

Like waves on the ocean's surface, they rocked back and forth, breaking into one another, both of them drowning in ecstasy. They both gave it all they could. Whatever their bodies had left to give; working toward the ultimate aim: supreme pleasure.

Teaq felt it creep up on him. Like a growing tension, simmering underneath the surface of his skin, until finally he could ignore it no longer.

Liliwen also was in the throes of desire, moaning with

each of his strokes, louder and louder, until she screamed out and dug her fingernails into his ass. "Oh yes! Oh yes, take me!"

He did.

With one final push, he claimed her. His inner wolf rejoiced.

Liliwen gasped for air, as did he.

Drained as he was, he sunk down on top of her and rested his head on her shoulder.

"You know I love you, right?" he whispered.

"As you should. I am your wife," she replied.

"That you are. And I am your man."

"Forever."

- THE END -

Shifters of Black Isle continues with *A Dragon's Treasure*, coming in November 2018.

About the Author

Dear Reader,

Thanks for reading *The Soldier and the Siren*. This is the second book in my brand new *Shifters of Black Isle* series, a collection of stories set in a fantasy world full of mystery, magic and fantastical creatures. I hope you're as excited about the rest of the series as I am!

I may have only released my first book in 2015, but I'm not new to writing in general. In fact, my mom still tells me to this day about how I would make up stories, and attempt to record them in my clumsy, shaky handwriting from the moment I learned to read and write. From there I went on to write fan fiction and other stuff meant for my own eyes only.

I've always enjoyed stories of the fantastic and paranormal. Vampires, shape shifters, witches and magic, all featured in the books I loved the most, even when I was still growing up. But it wasn't until much later that I got into romance. One of the first writers (an independent author just like me!) I came across was Tina Folsom, via her Scanguards

Vampire series. I was hooked. From there I went on to read more paranormal romance until I found a new kind of hero I loved: bear shifters, like the kind written by Milly Taiden, Zoe Chant, and T.S. Joyce. What I love about bears is how they can be all strong and independent, a bit reclusive, and almost grumpy, but they always end up having a heart of gold (plus they tend to know their food, and we all know that a man who can cook is doubly sexy). All that (except for the shifting into a powerful bear) almost exactly describes the sort of man I ended up falling for and marrying in real life, so it's no surprise that this is what I started my publishing career with.

To find out more, check:

LoreleiMoone.com (And why not sign up for the newsletter to be the first to find out about new releases.)

You can also get in touch with me via Facebook (search for Lorelei Moone), or email at info@loreleimoone.com

x Lorelei

HAVE YOU MET THE SCOTTISH WEREBEARS?

Before there was Alpha Squad, there were the Scottish Werebears… And if you sign up for Lorelei Moone's mailing list at loreleimoone.com, you get Book 1, Scottish Werebear: An Unexpected Affair absolutely free!

Titles in the Scottish Werebears series include:

An Unexpected Affair

A Dangerous Business

A Forbidden Love

A New Beginning

A Painful Dilemma

A Second Chance

These individual books in the Scottish Werebears series are best read in order. They can also be enjoyed as part of the Scottish Werebear: Complete Collection boxed set.

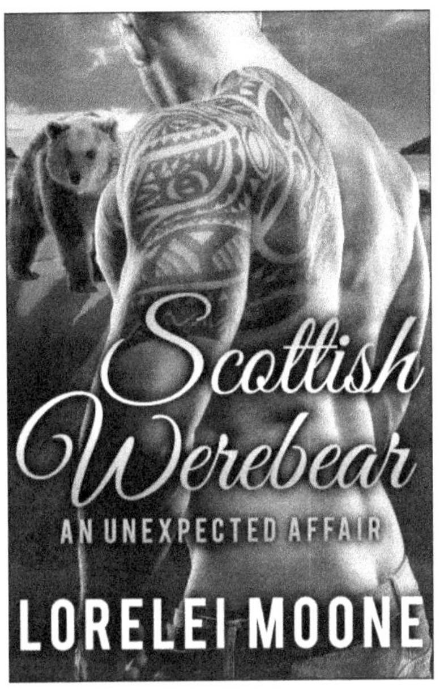

When romance novelist, Clarice Adler, hides herself away in a secluded holiday cottage to finish a book, the last thing she needs is another relationship. Imagine her surprise when she falls head over heels for the man who runs the place. Derek McMillan knows Clarice is his mate, but he's a bear shifter and she's human and the two simply don't mix. They are literally worlds apart; can they find a way to come together?

Get this book for free by joining Lorelei Moone's mailing list at loreleimoone.com!